She wanted to sleep with Quinn...

Not to beat around the bush or anything, but Annabel wanted to make love with him. Right now. Like crazy. The breakup with her ex weeks ago had left her alone, but satisfied. Usually it was six to eight months before she craved intimacy. But one glimpse of Quinn on her doorstep had her libido rising like a chocolate-Chambord soufflé.

"So your brother John tells me you need rescuing," he murmured.

Annabel's welcoming smile traded itself for a dropped jaw. "Rescuing?"

"He said you don't know how to have fun anymore." His eyes twinkled.

"Huh?"

Quinn cocked his head to one side and shot her an amused look. "Don't. Know. How. To. Have. Fun."

The overenunciation of each word brought her attention to his lips, which were full and all-male and magnificent. She could imagine him kissing every inch of her body. Why didn't he just strip her naked now and pleasure her till she screamed?

Because that would be fine. Really. And maybe even fun...

Blaze™

Dear Reader,

I've always loved the Charles Dickens story *A Christmas Carol*. It hit me one day that it would be fun to write a Christmas Blaze novel with a female "Scrooge" heroine. Of course, instead of three spirits, she has the sexy-as-hell and very real man from her past, Quinn Garrett, to guide her to her own salvation. Which he does in a highly sensual, won't-take-no fashion.

I'm also a big fan of reunion stories where couples who didn't get it right the first time manage to struggle through personal growth in round two and reach their happy-ever-after. In Annabel and Quinn's case, teenage unrequited love is given a second chance—this time with all the additional fun adults get to have.

Hope you enjoy the book! And if you lived a second-chance-at-teenage-love story, e-mail me through my Web site, www.IsabelSharpe.com. I'd love to hear it!

Cheers,

Isabel Sharpe

Books by Isabel Sharpe
HARLEQUIN BLAZE
11—THE WILD SIDE
76—A TASTE OF FANTASY
126—TAKE ME TWICE

Don't miss any of our special offers. Write to us at the following address for information on our newest releases.

Harlequin Reader Service
U.S.: 3010 Walden Ave., P.O. Box 1325, Buffalo, NY 14269
Canadian: P.O. Box 609, Fort Erie, Ont. L2A 5X3

Before I Melt Away

ISABEL SHARPE

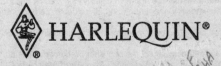

HARLEQUIN®

TORONTO • NEW YORK • LONDON
AMSTERDAM • PARIS • SYDNEY • HAMBURG
STOCKHOLM • ATHENS • TOKYO • MILAN • MADRID
PRAGUE • WARSAW • BUDAPEST • AUCKLAND

To Birgit,
with gratitude, respect and affection

ISBN 0-373-79166-6

BEFORE I MELT AWAY

Copyright © 2004 by Muna Shehadi Sill.

This edition published by arrangement with Harlequin Books S.A.

www.eHarlequin.com

Printed in U.S.A.

1

To: John Brightman
From: Quinn Garrett
Date: November 19
Subject: Long time no see
Hello, John. I googled your name and found your work e-mail. You're no longer in Wisconsin—big disappointment. I'm heading to Milwaukee in December to see about starting a manufacturing plant for the HC-3 and was hoping to see you. I have a lot of good memories of the year I spent with your family. Hope you are well.

   Quinn

To: Quinn Garrett
From: John Brightman
Date: November 20
Subject: Re: Long time no see
Quinn! How the hell are you? God, it's been forever! Sixteen years? Of course I've followed your rise to the top with Holocorp, so I know more about you than you do about me. I guess you're probably sick of comparisons to the big Gates guy, but if the shoe fits... Congratulations, you've done the world of

technology a lot of good. My students already act as if holographic computer screens have been in existence since the dawn of time.

I'm teaching at Rollins, still can't get used to the Florida climate. My sister is the only one left in Milwaukee; I'm sorry to say my parents passed on, Dad about six years ago, Mom two.

Look Annabel up when you're there. She started a personal chef business a year ago and is running herself ragged. Take her out and make her have some fun, for God's sake. You might be the great success story of the twenty-first century, but I can't believe you've forgotten how to have fun. She apparently has.

Will you be around at Christmastime or back in California? Or are you visiting your folks in Maine? I wasn't planning to come home; Annabel doesn't "do" Christmas anymore, but if you're there, maybe I will, and bring Alison and the kids. I've got a cousin who owns a house next to the lake and there's plenty of room.

Got to run to a class, stay in touch.

Best,

John

ANNABEL TURNED her minivan into her narrow driveway on Sixty-third Street in Wauwatosa, only three blocks west of the Milwaukee city line, pressed her garage-door opener and sailed into the two-car garage. Yes, indeed, she was fried like an egg. All day, cooking a week's worth of meals at the Bergers, the fussiest people on earth. Ted, one of the students she hired to help out, was cramming this week for his exams at Milwaukee Area Technical College, so Annabel had taken over at a time she'd rather be working on getting more new business. *Things might be going well, but they could be going better.* Her personal mantra.

This time of year was always nuts. Starting mid-November, people wanted to party instead of work. Which meant shifting from high gear to overdrive. Plus, in addition to her regular roster of clients and the extra holiday dinner parties, this year she was adding a new option—Dinner and a Show. Pairing an early dinner party at the client's home with tickets to *The Nutcracker* or *A Christmas Carol,* or a Milwaukee Symphony Holiday Pops Concert. Included in the deal was a limo chauffeuring the lucky paying guests to and from. Dessert and drinks after the show could be had in addition to or instead of dinner.

Brilliant, if she did say so herself, which she did and no apologies. With any luck she could get a real office someday and lose the stigma of the cute little woman starting a cute little business out of her home. Pat, pat, pat and a cheek pinch—yick.

If Annabel had anything to say about it, Chefs Tonight would be anything but cute. Chefs Tonight would someday be an empire. Her dishes would be delivered around the world, syndicated newspaper columns would feature her menus, her cookbooks, her recipes. She'd be the female version of Adolph Fox, the success comet whose tail she was following, the man who'd put his signature gourmet food in every supermarket freezer in the country.

She stepped out of her minivan—oh, for a sexy convertible, but sexy convertibles were bad news when it came to lugging clients' groceries around town—and grabbed her fancy leather briefcase, a gift to herself last summer when she signed on her tenth client.

Outside in the misty, damp December air, she jabbed the button to lower the garage door. It was unusually warm for this time of year, upper forties and densely foggy, ho, ho, ho, thanks a lot. The houses across the street appeared and disappeared as if they, not the fog, were undulating and immaterial.

The soles of her clogs clunked across cement to her back door, her footsteps louder than usual in the thick, silent air. She grabbed her keys and let herself into her house, kicked off the shoes and padded to the back bedroom her assistant used as an office.

"Hey, Stefanie. Any messages?" She glanced at the miniature lit Christmas tree on Stefanie's desk. "Very cute."

"How was it being back on the front lines today?" Stefanie smiled over from the holograph hovering above her desk, where she was entering in the dietary requirements of a new client. Her usually clear eyes looked puffy and bloodshot; her normally rosy skin was pale and blotchy, as if she hadn't slept well in days.

"Grueling. Like being back in school. But you know the Bergers. Meat-and-potatoes father, mother on the Atkins diet, son won't eat vegetables, daughter is vegan. No wonder Mom Berger hired us."

"No wonder." Stefanie yawned, rolled her chair to her desk and handed Annabel four pink message slips.

"Any new business queries today—I hope?" Annabel leafed through the messages and made a sound of exasperation. "Bob called *again?*"

"Three times in the last hour. The poor man is obviously *still* hoping you'll get back together. He said he wanted to catch you in and I shouldn't tell you he called." Stefanie rolled her eyes. "Like I wouldn't."

"Well, he's persistent, I'll give him that. What else?"

"Four phone queries, responding to the regular ad in the *Sentinel*. Five calling about Dinner and a Show and three e-mail responses."

"Any through our Web site?"

"No."

"Okay." Annabel glanced at the other messages— one from a downtown organization that wanted her to give a cooking demonstration for at-risk kids. Like she had the time? She handed that one back to Stefanie. "All in all, a good day. Say no to these people, send them a check. Fifty bucks should make them happy."

"Will do." Stefanie yawned again, guiltily covering her mouth. "Sorry, it's this weather. Four-thirty, getting dark already, and the fog makes me want to curl up and sleep forever."

"Ha! It's your space heater, roasting you soporific."

"I'd be a lump of ice without it." Stefanie shivered and rubbed her hands together over its warmth. "You must have been an Eskimo in another life."

"Cold is good for you." Annabel smiled and headed for her own office.

"Oh, someone else called, but didn't leave a message. Deep voice, totally dreamy-sounding. Said he wanted to surprise you."

"Really." Annabel paused in the hallway, frowning. Who would want to surprise her? "It wasn't John goofing off?"

"No. I'd know your brother's voice, even clowning around."

"Hmm. Okay. Probably another male who didn't quite get the meaning of 'it's over.'" She continued into her office, grinning at Stefanie's giggle. Running joke between them that Annabel had an army of men clawing to get back into her life. Right now that army consisted of: Bob, whom she'd dated briefly, though longer than most—three months—before she got restless. Or bored. Or just too busy.

When she went looking for a man, she wanted her sexual itch scratched, a warm body to provide company for a while, then to leave so she could work on business until the urge struck again.

She was always up-front about what she wanted and they all reacted with the same patronizing nod, and the same gleam in their eyes that said they knew it was only a matter of time before their irresistible masculinity got her in touch with her inner need to be enslaved.

Strangely enough, it never had. Oh, my. Gasp of surprise and horror. A traitor to her gender she must be.

The look of bemused shock on the men's faces when she broke it off was identical, too. Impossible for them to comprehend that a woman didn't see her salvation in the form of a man. Ball-breaker, bitch, slut—she'd been called them all, and worse. When all along she'd been nothing but honest about where the relationship would end up and what she wanted it for.

Even more ironic, if she'd been one of their male buddies, they'd admire her. *Hey, dude, there's someone who got it right. Hot babes when he needs them, dumps them when he's done, no entanglements, no strings.* But she was a woman, and they didn't like seeing their own behavior reflected back.

Tough. Like a turkey roasted too long. This worked for her.

She went into her office, enjoying the clean, sleek look of the cream-colored walls, beige carpet and honey-maple furniture. The furniture had been an indulgence, but what was the point in buying cheap things that wouldn't last?

None. Why buy jarred caviar when you could save up for fresh and be sixty times happier, even if you could only eat it a quarter as often? You still came out ahead.

The phone rang; she waited for Stefanie to pick it up, curious about the deep-voiced man. Raoul had a pretty deep voice. But he'd long since married and would have no reason to call. Peter—maybe, but they'd parted badly. David, ditto.

Stefanie exchanged warm Christmas wishes with the caller, then clicked the hold button.

"Annabel, it's your cousin Linda."

"Oh, no." Annabel braced herself and picked up her phone. Either Linda had more questions about her husband, Evan's, holiday business party, which Chefs Tonight was preparing again this year, or, as every year, the same invitation—*We're having a Christmas party, hope you can join us.* Sweet of her, but Christmas was one of the few days this time of year that Annabel could avoid anything that involved either preparing food or parties. Her idea of Christmas heaven was staying in bed all day, watching movies and eating junk food. "Hi, Linda."

"Hey, Annabel. How's business going?" Linda's voice always sounded as if she was about to laugh, was laughing, or had just stopped. Annabel had a perfectly well-evolved sense of humor, but she would never understand what Linda found funny every second of the day.

"Business is booming, thanks." She kept her answer short, knowing Linda didn't really want all the details of how her business was going, and because they'd talked only last month about Evan's party. "How are Evan and the kids?"

Okay, so she asked. She had to ask. But Linda didn't realize that Annabel wanted to hear about Linda's kids exactly as much as Linda wanted to hear about Annabel's business.

After three minutes of detailed descriptions of each child—how many were there, a hundred by now?—his or her activities, clothing, cute antics, new words, Annabel couldn't take it anymore.

"So then Lawrence was sitting there, *covered* in yogurt and I—"

"Linda, I'm so sorry to interrupt you, but I have another call I have to take. Was there anything you wanted to talk about for Evan's party?"

Linda laughed as if Annabel was the wittiest person she'd ever met. "Oh, no. I just want to invite you to our annual Christmas Party. Four o'clock Christmas Day, by then the kids are all—"

"Oh, gosh, Linda, that's a bad day for me."

"But it's *Christmas*. You shouldn't be working, you should be spending time surrounded by loved ones. That's what the season is about."

"Sorry, Linda. I really am."

"Annabel, I worry about you, all closeted up with your business. We're family. You need to be with us, celebrating."

"Don't worry about me. I'm happy as a clam. On the half shell. With shallot vinaigrette and a touch of hot pepper."

Linda chuckled. "No way I can convince you? I just hate thinking of you sitting there by yourself on such a wonderful day."

"Trust me, sitting here by myself is what I love most about Christmas."

Linda sighed, for once not sounding like a sitcom laugh track. "Well, if you change your mind, please come. We send you our blessings of the season."

"Thanks." Annabel hung up the phone. Blessings of the season? What blessings? That she was so maniacally busy she could barely see straight? Not that she'd at all prefer the alternative.

"I'm going home." Stefanie appeared in the doorway, leaned against the jamb and yawned.

"See you tomorrow, bright and early. Ted's taking the Moynahans as usual, right?"

"Yes. He had a final this morning, he can do tomorrow."

"Good. Get some rest, you look exhausted."

"Oh, I'm fine. Just tired. Good night."

Annabel waved her out the door and settled down to read the newspaper's business section, looking for any possible—

Phone. Scowling, she picked it up. It was probably—

"Bob here."

Yep. "Hi, Bob."

"Did I call at a bad time?"

"You know me, I'm always busy."

"Yeah, no kidding."

"What's up?" She kept her voice brisk.

"Well…how've you been?"

"Did you want something?"

"I was wondering, if you'd like to—"

"Bob…" She rested her head on her hand.

"Meet me for coffee, that's it."

"No."

"I just want to—"

"We've been through this. And through this. And when we were done going through this, we went through this some more."

"I'm not trying to come on to you. I'm calling as a friend. I have this—"

"I'm sorry." She hung up the phone, slightly sick over her behavior. She'd tried niceness. Then firmness. Now it seemed out-and-out bitchiness might be the only thing he'd respond to.

Back to the business section. Nothing interesting in the news, nothing triggering any new ideas. She stuffed the paper into the blue recycling bag and went online to the Metro Milwaukee Association of Commerce site to check for new events she should attend to maximize networking. The one next week she knew about…nothing else looked—

Knock at her door. Grimacing, she stalked into the hallway and down the steps to the back. A short, sweet-faced middle-aged woman smiled up at her. "Hello, Annabel."

Annabel blinked. "Hi."

"I'm Kathy. Your neighbor across the street."

Duh. "Kathy, I'm so sorry. I was thinking…that is I was working, and my brain was…" She made a helpless gesture.

"I understand. I'm asking for donations for the cancer society. And to see if you could spare some time to—"

"Anything but time." Annabel ushered Kathy in. "I'll get my checkbook."

"Thank you. Are you coming to the Christmas Eve block party?" Kathy's smile turned pitying when she registered Annabel's blank look. "The invitations went around last month."

"Oh. No. I'm…busy that day, sorry."

"Too bad. It's a nice way to meet neighbors."

True, if she had any desire to meet her neighbors, that would be a nice way. "I'm sure."

She signed the check, handed it over to Kathy's profuse thanks, and ushered her out the door when Kathy showed signs of wanting to linger and chat. Back in her office, Annabel grabbed a small stack of résumés from students at MATC. If the Dinner and a Show program went well, she should be in a position to hire more help. More help doing the work in people's kitchens meant more of Annabel's time freed up to generate new business. *Things might be going well, but they could be going—*

Doorbell. Back door again. She groaned and went to answer, hoping for a nice package or letter dropped at her door that she could pick up and bring inside without having to interact with anyone.

No package. A bunch of kids, probably from the neighborhood. Who—oh, no—started to sing, the worst, most off-key rendition of "Frosty the Snowman" ever heard by man or beast. The first verse was pretty cute, but when they showed signs of gearing up for verse two, she thanked them firmly and shut the door.

Apparently privacy in her own home was too much to ask.

Back into her office, a few e-mails, some correspondence...she was getting hungry. The very fact of life that made her business possible—that bodies needed regular feeding—could often be an inconvenient interruption.

An hour and a half later, papers spread out on her kitchen table, she'd eaten the rest of a decent beef-cabbage soup and the other half of a grilled chicken sandwich taken home the night before from Carter's, her usual dinner spot. She'd also worked up a few ideas for their diabetic menu choices, and had an inspiration for a carb-free burger with artichoke bottoms instead of a bun for their Atkins selections. Substitute a portobello mushroom for the beef, and add it to their vegetarian menu.

Good work. After she cleaned up, she'd surf the net to see if anything new struck her for a Valentine's Day special that would bring in more business after the big holiday rush subsided. And she needed to figure out how to lure more traffic to the Web site. Oh, and tomorrow she had a dinner party to cook for in the evening over on the East Side; she'd need to remind herself to get the fish in the morning from Empire Seafood.

Dishes done, she stepped into her clogs, grabbed the full garbage bag and hauled it outside to the receptacle behind the house. Started back in, then remembered she'd forgotten to check her mail, not that it was anything but catalogs at this time of year.

She walked briskly down the driveway in fog so thick it felt like a clammy attempt at a drizzle, with streetlights illuminating the mist like spools of glow-in-the-dark cotton candy. The eerie silence on the street was broken only by her steps—impossibly loud, as if the sound waves were trapped, bouncing between the stone houses on the block like the ball in video Ping-Pong.

The temperature was supposed to drop radically tonight, possible snow predicted in the next few days. Oh, how not lovely. But that was Wisconsin in December. She pushed impatiently at her rapidly dampening hair and climbed three steps to her front door, heavy stained wood with an overly large brass knocker.

A breeze blew up suddenly, cold and damp. A glance over her shoulder showed the swirling fog lifting slightly, exposing the street. She crossed her arms over her chest and rubbed them, elbow to shoulder. Creepy night. She started to lean toward her mailbox, when a black flash of movement reflected off the knocker. Annabel whirled around and scanned behind her.

Nothing.

Strange. She reached again for her mail—yes, catalogs, catalogs and more catalogs—when a sound…or was it just a feeling?…made her freeze again. Was someone watching her? She had the distinct impression of a presence nearby, of eyes on her. Her own eyes flicked over to the knocker, searching again for the brief reflected movement.

Still nothing. Then a noise. Annabel whirled around again. A footstep?

Annabel.

She gasped and put her hand to her hammering heart. God, for a second she even thought she heard her name whispered out there in the darkness. Was she losing it? The fog was creepy, but come on. Who the hell was going to be loitering around her house, whispering her name, a ghost? A squirrel or a cat, or someone's pet had made a noise and her imagination cut loose, that was all. *Sheesh, get a grip.*

She put the catalogs under her arm when she spotted something definitely not good. Her door stood open, just a crack, but open.

Steady. Her heart pounded harder; she swallowed with difficulty. Stefanie had been fairly spacey the past few weeks; she might have forgotten to close it.

The wood felt cool and slightly damp under her fingertips as she pushed it open and went inside. In the living room, she paused, ears straining. No noise. Nothing looked disturbed. She went through the house, approaching each room with caution.

Nothing.

Okay, she was satisfied no one had been here who wasn't supposed to be. Stefanie must have left the door open. The spooky weather had set off Annabel's fear.

Back downstairs, she relocked both doors. Then for good measure, she checked that the first-floor windows were locked, too.

Good. Back to normal. Weirdness dispelled. Maybe to add warmth, she'd light a fire in her kinky fireplace— the tiles around the hearth had been painted and installed by the house's previous occupant. At first glance, innocent decoration. But a close look showed various couples enjoying various acts of…non-innocence.

Annabel loved them.

She crumpled newspaper, added kindling, and one log—why bother with more when she'd only be here briefly?

While the fire caught, she turned the heat down to

sixty, turned on the outside lights and went up to her room. Changed into her bright red pajamas, brushed her teeth, washed her face, and took two cooking magazines back downstairs. So she could research while enjoying the flickering flames.

Six fairly dull articles later—how to make the perfect holiday centerpiece…what, to distract from bad food?—the breeze that started lifting the fog earlier had become a serious wind, rattling her windows and moaning through the crack under the front door. Annabel shivered. Wind was a restless, roaming, angry force and it made her want to bury herself under her blankets and pillow the way she had when she was a child. Thunder and lightning, no problem. Hail, ditto. But strong winds, no thanks. One tornado-producing storm had roared through her childhood and blown into her a healthy fear of that power.

The fire all but out, she beat a hasty childish retreat upstairs into her room. By that time, the gusts had died down a bit and another sound rose up, a clanking rattle, as if someone was dragging metal down the street.

She laughed uneasily and shook her head. So now her ghost had chains? How clichéd.

The wind picked up again, the rattling came closer, then an unearthly howl competed with the gusting blasts.

"Oh, for—" Annabel leaped to the window. This was starting to feel like the setup to a horror movie, and it was giving her the heebie-jeebies.

She yanked aside the curtain and pulled up the shade, determined to find normal and comforting explanations.

Ha. Just as she thought. The howling was Elsa, the beagle next door. Clanking chains—she scanned the street. Hmm.

Wait... Annabel squinted and pressed her forehead to the glass. Across the street, a man was jacking up his car. *Ta-da.* Clanking metal equaled jack being dragged around the car. Aha. Nothing like the delightful dullness of everyday explanations for her fears.

She stayed at the window and watched the man working, squatted in the street next to his flat tire. He had on a long dark dress coat, unusual in this neighborhood, where most of the men wore casual parkas.

The headlights of an oncoming car caught him; he turned his head and stood to get out of the way. Annabel registered a strong nose, nice profile, dark hair ruffling in the wind. He looked vaguely familiar.

The car passed, leaving the man in darkness again, except for the glow of the streetlight in front of Annabel's house, no longer so shrouded by fog. She watched, waiting for the man to crouch and continue working.

Instead, he turned and looked directly up at her, as if he'd known she was standing there. Annabel gasped and instinctively lunged out of sight, then stood in the shadow of her curtain, hand pressed against her chest. He looked familiar straight on, too, but she couldn't place him. Someone she had met at an after-hours event? She went over his features in her memory, trying to imagine him with a drink in his hand, or sitting in a lecture hall, or at a family dining table while she served dinner.

No luck. But she knew him, no question.

On impulse, she yanked down the shades, turned the lights out in her room and crept back to the window, folding back the edge of the shade just the tiniest bit so she could peek without being silhouetted by the light in her room.

He was gone.

She blinked and searched the area around his car. Nothing. Nowhere. Vanished.

Okay, the night was getting even weirder now.

Forget it. Back to bed, to *Gourmet* and *Food & Wine*. He probably gave up on the tire and went into his car to dial roadside assistance.

She'd settled back into her bed and picked up her magazine when her front doorbell rang, followed by the sharp metallic rapping of the knocker.

2

ANNABEL FROZE. Who the hell was ringing her doorbell at—she glanced at the clock—ten-seventeen on a week-night? She got out of bed and went to the window, strained to see if any sign of the caller was visible. No. He or she must be standing too close to the door; the roof obstructed Annabel's view.

Okay. So how stupid was it for a woman living alone to answer the door at night?

Pretty stupid.

She grabbed a robe from her closet, jammed her feet into her ratty black slippers and started downstairs, unable to resist her curiosity. Was it the man fixing his tire? Maybe he needed to use her phone? Except what kind of person didn't own a cell nowadays?

The bell rang once more, followed again by the rapping knocker. Impatient type. She hurried through her dining room, living room, then opened the door into the always chilly front entranceway. "Who is it?"

"Annabel. It's Quinn Garrett."

Annabel's eyes shot wide; her mouth dropped open to emit incredulous laughter. Quinn. She should have recognized him immediately. Even if she couldn't place him from the year he spent with her family on a high-school exchange program, she should have recognized him from the media fuss over the years. Newspaper, magazines, TV, the guy had become a household name—just not one she expected to show up on her street.

"Quinn!" She eagerly opened the door, then had to steel herself not to take a step back.

Yes, she'd seen that he grew up even more gorgeous than he'd been in high school. Lost the boyish roundness to his face, and the teenage awkwardness. But she was totally unprepared for the impact of seeing him in the flesh, totally unprepared for the intense buzz of chemistry—on her end anyway. Holy cheezits. She'd had a crush on him all those years ago, but the physical reaction was extremely different now that she knew what all those fluttery feelings meant.

"Annabel." His voice was even more resonant coming to her live and in person, his eyes dark and intense; she could barely keep her gaze on his.

"Hi," she said oh-so-brilliantly, sounding breathless and starstruck—not at all a coincidence, since she was both. "Quinn," she added even more brilliantly.

His lips curved in a smile. "You grew up."

"Oh. Yes." She winced. Maybe try saying something intelligent? "So did you."

Good job.

"I guess that makes two of us." He grinned suddenly, a full white-toothed grin, which made him so sexy she feared hyperventilation. "I was planning to show up at a more reasonable hour, but when I saw you at your window, I thought I might as well say hello now."

"Can I help?" She gestured out at his car, probably a rental—Lexus?

"Just a flat. All fixed."

"Very good." She moved aside in the doorway. "Come in."

"Are you sure? You were on your way to bed." He glanced at her robe, making her so not happy she'd grabbed the thick flowery one that had pills all over it. She'd much rather be wearing silk. Or even better, clothes. She felt vulnerable and strange like this, even though he'd seen her in her pajamas dozens of times. But then that was years ago; she'd been thirteen and hardly the stuff of male fantasy. More like an annoying little sister.

She did not want him to see her as an annoying little sister now.

He took off his coat and the white, probably cashmere, scarf, and, oh, my God, he was wearing a tux. Even homely looked good in a tux; gorgeous should be outlawed.

"I was at a party in Brookfield—I'm a little overdressed."

"I'm a little underdressed."

"So we even out." He stood, hands on his hips pushing back his jacket, clearly at ease in her living room, while she had to remind herself not to fidget.

"Have a seat." She indicated the couch behind him. "Can I get you something to drink?"

"Water would be nice."

"That's all? I have cider, wine, beer, cognac…"

He held up a hand to stop her list. "Water is really what I want."

"Water coming up." She padded into the kitchen, feeling round and unappealing, wondering if it would be weird to go upstairs and throw on some clothes. Maybe a thong and a push-up bra? Or, okay, jeans and a nice tight sweater, too. But if she did that, he'd know she was uncomfortable around him this way, which would make things even more uncomfortable.

She ran the water until it was good and cold, filled a glass, poured Dove dark chocolate pieces, dried apricots and plain-roasted almonds into small brass bowls and put them on a wooden tray. Water might be what he wanted, but the professional hostess in her had to offer more.

"Here you go." She smiled too brightly and headed toward him, feeling even rounder and less appealing when she saw how amazing he looked sitting on her couch, bow tie untied, collar button undone, arm up along the back of the sofa. *GQ* much? Of course, he'd probably been on their cover, probably more than once. It was so hard to reconcile the kid she'd known with this…well, look up *male* in the dictionary and find his picture.

He reached for the glass and lifted a dark brow at the tray of food. "With trimmings?"

"I am unable to serve only water to my guests. It's become genetically impossible." She perched on a chair across the narrow room. If she were dressed to match his trappings, she'd have no problem sitting next to him on the couch. Leaning close. Closer. Closest. Straddling him and…okay, enough.

"I remember being extremely well fed at your house. Your mom was a great cook. I'm sorry to hear she and your dad died."

"Thanks." Annabel's voice dropped low in her throat. "I miss them."

"They were great people. Your whole family. That year was really special for me."

"Us, too." She smiled, then almost wished she hadn't when he caught her eyes and held on, and the tension stretched to nearly unbearable.

Not to beat around the bush or anything, but she wanted to sleep with him. Like crazy. The breakup with Bob weeks ago had left her alone, but satisfied. Usually it was six to eight months before she wanted to start in again. But one glimpse of this man had her libido rising like a chocolate Chambord soufflé.

"So, your brother John tells me you need rescuing."

Annabel's smile traded itself for a dropped jaw. "Excuse me? Rescuing?"

"He said you don't know how to have fun anymore."

"Huh?"

He cocked his head back to one side and shot her an amused look from under his lids. "Don't. Know. How. To. Have. Fun."

The overenunciation of each word of course brought her attention to his lips, which were full and all male and magnificent and why didn't he just strip naked now and pleasure her until she screamed?

Because that would be fine. Really.

"Tell my brother John that I *know* how to have fun."

He moved casually, adjusting his position on the couch, but his eyes were on her like a frog watching the bug soon to be glued to its tongue.

And oh, what a lovely image that was.

"How do you have fun?"

A flush rose to Annabel's cheeks. She so wanted to answer that question in a very provocative and enticing way. But not while she was wearing bright red flannel pajamas and a robe that made her look like Mrs. Claus first thing in the morning. Besides, women must try to get into Quinn Garrett's pants all day long. Inspiring all that lust probably got tedious. Not to mention that she'd been sort of a sister to him all those years ago, which might still be how he thought of her.

Bummer. Major bummer.

"When I want to have fun, I go out."

"Where?"

"To restaurants, movies, clubs…" Okay, not clubs; noise and smoke were not her thing, but it sounded good.

"With whom?"

Whoever I'm boinking at the moment. "Dates."

"When was the last time?"

"Is this an interrogation? Should I move the lamp so it shines in my eyes?"

"No." He leaned on the sofa arm, index finger resting against his temple, fingers curled next to his mouth.

Bond. James Bond. Double-oh—

"When was the last time you went out and had fun?"

"Well, that was…" Annabel frowned. No fair. She broke up with Bob officially a month ago, and she hadn't seen much of him for a week or two before that since she'd been so busy. "Probably not as long ago as it sounds."

"That's what I thought." He drained his glass, put it carefully back on the coaster on her cherry coffee table and leaned forward, forearms on his knees. Immediately she wanted to copycat lean-forward, too. Even though he was sitting across the room, the gesture brought him closer enough—brought those killer eyes closer enough—that it felt intimate.

Damn the pilly robe.

"So what are you doing in Milwaukee?" With any luck he wouldn't notice that she'd changed the sub—

"Changing the subject?"

Damn. "Okay, you got me."

He started a smile, didn't let it get far. "I'm here as decoration, mostly. We're hoping to buy the old Herrn brewery and start manufacturing HC-3s here in Milwaukee. Other people do the talking, the negotiating, I show up and act like I'm important."

"I imagine you are."

"You always had a good imagination."

She chuckled, foolishly pleased he referred to their history, that he'd bothered to remember her. Or was doing a damn good job faking it. "We could use that kind of industry here. You'll be doing the city a lot of good."

"That's the idea. I have a soft spot for Milwaukee, for obvious reasons."

Annabel smiled graciously as his comment warranted, but she was thinking he probably didn't have a soft spot anywhere.

How depraved was she to meet an old friend unexpectedly and want nothing more than to see him naked? "What brought you to this neighborhood tonight? You said you were at a party in Brookfield?"

"Spur-of-the-moment decision driving back. I wanted to see where you lived. Then my tire went, practically at your door and you know the rest."

"It was funny, with the wind, dog howling next door,

your jack clanking on the street—I thought I was being haunted."

He narrowed his eyes for a fleeting second, then got up abruptly, approached her fireplace and crouched to examine the tiles. "Excuse me, but I have to see if these are what I think."

"They are." She laughed, a little nervously, willing the heat to stay out of her cheeks. How many people had she shown those pictures off to? *Now* she wanted to blush? "An artist used to live here, who apparently had a rather liberal view of life. But I like them. They're not obvious unless you look closely. You're the first person who spotted them on his own."

"Am I?" His eyebrows went up, but she had the feeling he wasn't surprised. She shouldn't be, either. Even in high school, nothing had escaped his notice. Of course, that fact would have made no impression on her at thirteen, except that her parents kept commenting on what a remarkable boy he was. A remarkable boy who'd grown into a remarkable man. Damn shame Mom and Dad weren't here to see it. Her mom especially had doted on Quinn, and missed him when he went back home, though she'd loved that he kept in touch for several years, especially at Christmas.

"Why the sadness?"

Annabel started. He hadn't even glanced at her, she was sure. He was standing now, staring into the fireplace where her lone log still glowed orange underneath. Freaky how he did that. More than once when she'd been in thirteen-year-old hormone hell, he'd understood what she was feeling more than her parents had. Or so it seemed to her at the time.

"I was thinking Mom and Dad would have really liked to know you now."

"Maybe they do."

She shot him a startled look, then laughed. "I suppose that's possible."

He picked up a tiny framed print from her mantel, *Three Spirits Mad With Joy,* by Warwick Goble, a whimsical favorite of hers left to her by her mom. "I used to think the dead should be allowed to come back one day a year, to see the people who miss them."

"You don't anymore?"

He turned, cocking his head in a silent question.

"You said *used* to think."

"Oh." He put the picture down. "I guess I hadn't thought about it in a while."

"Who would you want to come back?"

"Sally." He spoke without hesitation.

Annabel clenched her teeth against irrational jealousy. She hadn't read about him getting married or being attached, but then Quinn Garrett was adamant about keeping his personal life away from the press. "I'm sorry. Someone special?"

"Very."

"Girlfriend?"

"Guinea pig."

Annabel burst out laughing. "Be serious."

"I am serious. I had her when I was a boy. She listened to everything I said, never thought I was odd. It was always clear what she wanted from me." He chuckled, reminding Annabel how seldom he laughed out loud.

"She sounds wonderful. Who else would you want to come back? I hope your parents are still in this world."

"Mom is." He moved back to the couch to grab his coat. Even in high school he'd been reluctant to discuss his life or his parents. All she knew was that they lived in Hartland, Maine—sister city to Hartland, Wisconsin, where Annabel had grown up, and that his father had worked at a tannery while mom stayed home.

"I should go."

"You should?" She stood up, absurdly disappointed, and followed him into the chilly front entranceway.

"I've taken up too much of your evening already."

She stopped herself from offering him the rest of it, wanting to ask *Will I see you again?* but hating the clingy-woman line. "Thank you for stopping by."

"I'll see you again."

She couldn't help the wide smile. "I'd like that."

"I would, too." He leaned forward and for one crazy second, she thought he was going to kiss her and her entire being went on hold. Then he stopped several inches away and she had to use everything in her power not to look disappointed.

"I'm counting on you to show me some fun while I'm here, Annabel." His eyes were warm, bottomless, and he smelled like expensive male heaven.

Oh, yes. "How long will you be here?"

"As long as it takes."

"To negotiate the acquisition?"

He lifted one eyebrow briefly, then leaned the rest of the way toward her and kissed her…

On the cheek, oh crap.

"I'll call you tomorrow." He let himself out and strode down her front walk toward his car.

Annabel shut the door slowly, not wanting him to

turn and catch her mooning after him but reluctant to cut herself off from the sight of him. Her heart was pounding, cheeks flushed, body buzzing with excitement in spite of her disappointment. She'd see him again. When she wasn't wearing pajamas.

Across the street, she heard his car door open, close, the engine start up and drive slowly away.

She'd be wearing nothing like pajamas. Nothing to remind him of the year when she'd been practically his little sister. Then maybe his next kiss goodbye wouldn't be aimed at her cheek.

And maybe, just maybe, it would last all night.

THE PHONE RANG. Annabel's eyes shot open.

Early. Very early. Her body could tell. Who was calling? Had something happened? She'd been dreaming— a curtain around her bed, some menace approaching, about to yank it back…

She reached for the phone, glancing at the clock. Six o'clock. If Ted was trying to worm out of cooking for the Moynahans today, she'd kill him.

"Annabel."

The adrenaline that had kicked in at her abrupt awakening doubled. No, tripled.

"Quinn." She pitched her voice higher than usual so he wouldn't hear the sleep still in it.

"I woke you."

Annabel rolled her eyes. She couldn't get anything past the man. "It's okay."

"Have breakfast with me."

"I can't." The words came to her lips before she'd even thought them through.

A low chuckle on the line. "Let's try that again. Have breakfast with me, Annabel."

This time the request, or rather command, sneaked past her Automatic Self-Denial System—was it the sexy way he said her name?—and she found she really wanted to. But she had so much to—

"Café at the Pfister. At seven."

She smiled and fell back onto the bed, one hand holding the phone to her ear, the other pushing her hair back. Could she? A quick shower, dressing for him in actual clothes, a quick fifteen-minute drive downtown, breakfast for an hour or so, back here ready to go by eight-thirty or nine—not that much past her usual time. And it might be her only chance to see Quinn again; the man was doubtless booked solid while he was here. Everyone must want a piece of him.

Okay, she was convinced.

"That sounds fine."

"See you then."

He signed off and she threw back the covers, bounded from the bed and shed her pajamas on the way to the shower. Fifteen minutes later, washed, dried, lotioned and deodorized, she stood in front of her closet, awash in an unfamiliar emotion: indecision.

There was only one outfit she knew she wasn't going to wear, and that was the one she'd just picked up off the floor and tossed back onto her bed. But what? Sexy? Businesslike? Formal? Casual?

No jeans at the Pfister, Milwaukee's grand old hotel. And she was sick of won't-show-or-hold-stains pants and shirts for work at clients' homes. But the all-business suits she wore to networking events…so cold, so...not seductive. Not that she wanted to be blatant about it. But hell, she was single, he was single; consenting adults could create many hot, appetizing scenarios if all the ingredients came together properly. She'd certainly love to taste what he was made of. And while she wouldn't go as far as throwing herself at him, looking female wouldn't hurt.

She settled on a red suit with a knee-length skirt and plunging V-collar jacket, nipped in at the waist. Under it a black stretch camisole with built-in bra. Silver earrings, a silver chain, plain stockings and high black pumps, which always felt confining and wobbly after so much time in clogs and slippers.

There. Not too conservative, not too sexy. And it was breakfast, after all, not dancing by moonlight.

Oh, but that was a nice thought, too.

Makeup next—not too much on her still-sleepy face or risk looking like a professional escort, ahem. Mascara, blush, red lipstick blotted down to a respectable level of brightness, under-eye concealer. Was it her imagination or did she need more of that every year as she neared thirty? A wrinkled-nose look at her nails. No way could she keep polish on with all the chopping and scrubbing she did in her job. Ah, well. She was more than the sum total of her manicure.

Glance in the mirror—okay, who was she kidding, a long, careful study—and she was ready. To have breakfast with Quinn. Oh my, yes.

In her unsexy minivan, she drove Route 41 to I 94, past the Brewers Stadium, past the sour-mash-and-hops smell of the Miller brewery, then off the highway and in among the buildings and asphalt of downtown, over on

Wisconsin Avenue to Jefferson, circling the nineteenth-century, green-awninged Pfister and into the hotel's garage.

Her heels made important-sounding click-clacks down the ramp, then tap-tapped into the elevator to the first floor and went quiet on the lobby carpet into the café.

She mentioned Quinn's name unnecessarily to the maître-d'—unnecessarily, because within a heartbeat of being inside the restaurant, she saw him. Couldn't help seeing him. He stuck out among the other suited men in the room, even though there was no immediately definable reason why he should, other than that he was familiar. But it went beyond that, if the glances from other diners were anything to go by, beyond even his celebrity. The man radiated...sex. No, he radiated power and authority and grace. And if you happened to find those traits sexy—and who didn't?—then yes, you could say he radiated sex. Which she just did say. Not that she was repeating herself because she was flustered...or anything.

He stood and watched her coming toward their table, apparently at ease with eye contact since they were out of speaking range, which made most people busy themselves with glancing at watches or fussing with silverware.

She neared the table and said hello, beaming goofily; she couldn't help it. He said hello back and sat only after she'd parked her butt opposite. Funny how she never noticed men's badly fitting suits, but she sure noticed one that fit well. It didn't just hang on him, or fight his movements. It rested and breathed with him, sat perfectly when he did. It would look *so* wonderful draped over a chair after he'd taken it off for the purpose of thrashing around with...okay, she had to stop that.

"I'm glad you decided to join me."

"I got the impression you wouldn't have let me refuse."

"True." He gave that implied smile and picked up a menu. "If you said no, I was going to show up at your house with bagels and coffee."

"A man who gets what he wants."

He regarded her with an enigmatic expression that made her want to x-ray his brain and see what was going on inside. "I've been reading a biography of Napoleon. That man had a hunger for power and acquisitions that could never be satisfied."

"After you're crowned emperor, what's left?"

"Exactly. Sometimes I get what I want. But I always want what I get. It's enough."

"Admirable." She picked up her menu, thinking he might as well call himself emperor. He'd single-handedly revolutionized the PC, the industry, and practically the world. It was a no-brainer he had enough. While she was still struggling to get her business off the ground.

"Easy for me to say?"

Annabel blinked up from Lighter Fare. "How do you do that?"

"What?"

"Read my mind."

He gave a slow grin. "I invented a mind reader, too, didn't you hear? Little chip, implanted in my temple."

She laughed, thinking that the familiar comfort of having known him a long time ago, contrasted with grown-up sexual edginess, made their chemistry even harder to resist. "Ah, so that's how you do it."

"Most people would be thinking the same thing. That

it's easy for me to say I'm satisfied, when to all appearances I have everything."

"Probably." She didn't want to go into the fact that he seemed to be able to read her mind when she couldn't possibly be thinking what everyone else would be thinking.

"So maybe I am perceived as the emperor now. But I was satisfied when I was working for Microsoft. And I was satisfied when my start-up company netted thirty thousand annually—when the HC-1 was considered a novelty sci-fi gimmick that would never catch on. So I'd like to think wanting what I get is a true philosophy."

"Very Zen of you." She picked up her water glass and took a sip, not entirely convinced. People happy with less didn't generally end up with so much more.

"But I have to tell you something even more important than my life's philosophy."

She put her glass down. "What's that?"

"You are incredibly beautiful all grown-up, Annabel."

All grown-up Annabel was very glad she wasn't still holding the glass, because at his comment it would have slipped from her fingers and crashed all over the lovely table. Oh, did that sound wonderful coming from him.

"Thank you." Her cheeks grew warm. "You're pretty spectacular all grown-up, too."

"Thank you." He, of course, didn't blush. His self-control was absolute. And yes, she'd love to make him lose it.

"Can I take your order?" The matronly waitress stood at the table, bowing slightly forward, as if in the presence of royalty.

Annabel glanced longingly at the skillet breakfast on the menu, but if she started her day with that much heavy food, she'd want to crawl in bed and stay, and she had a lot to accomplish. "I'd like the yogurt-and-fruit parfait, orange juice and tea, please."

"Smoked-salmon bagel, no cream cheese, grapefruit juice and coffee." Quinn handed his menu to the waitress, who actually did bow before she swept away.

"Tell me about your business, Annabel." He turned those magnificent eyes back on her. It was true what people said, that when Quinn Garrett spoke to you, he made you feel no one else existed. She'd just like to know he was genuinely feeling that way with her.

"I'm a personal chef. I do your grocery shopping, come into your home on a day you choose, cook a week's worth of meals from menus you select, package, freeze and clean up the whole shebang."

"Wow. Where do I sign up?"

She smiled, and let the eye contact go a little too long, just for the cheap thrill. "I will also come into your home, cook, serve and clean up your dinner party—sit-down or buffet."

"Maybe I'll hire you while I'm here. My place has a fairly decent kitchen."

Her heart leaped, for professional reasons this time. Quinn would no doubt be entertaining high-powered Milwaukee elite. She could make some valuable contacts. "You're not at the hotel?"

He shook his head. "I've rented a furnished apartment."

"So you're staying on for a while?"

"It looks that way."

She was so pleased she actually laughed. "Oh, that's great."

The waitress arrived with juice, leaving Annabel's gushing enthusiasm hanging in the silence between them.

Fawn on, little sister.

Quinn nodded his thanks to the waitress, then fixed Annabel with his dark brown eyes again. "I want to see a lot of you while I'm here."

Oh, my. It was on the tip of her tongue to say *You can see all of me,* but she thought that was a little grossly eager. "I'd like that."

"Good." He sat back as if satisfied the deal had been cemented.

Annabel gave herself a figurative smack out of fantasyland. See a lot of her? Hello? Do we have lots of time to be lollygagging around with *People* magazine's *Sexiest Man Alive?*

"Though actually, I'm pretty crazy busy at this time of year. People want to party, so the holidays are my most profitable time."

"We'll work it out."

Absolute confidence. Annabel leaned back to give the waitress room to set down breakfast. That's what made people like Quinn—and Napoleon—succeed. She was confident her business would do well, but not *absolutely* confident. She needed to ratchet that up a few notches, get herself in a position of more security so she could—

"I assume your nights are free."

The spoonful of yogurt made it only halfway to Annabel's mouth. "My nights?"

"Yes." He glanced up calmly from his bagel, on which he was arranging salmon, tomato slices and capers, a combination she'd already filed away in her mental recipe holder. "How much sleep do you need?"

"I...not much. Five or six hours."

"Then we'll have nights together."

Stay away, blush, stay the hell away. Did he mean... what did he mean? Did his—

He reached across the table, laid his finger against her lips, shushing her, even though she hadn't said anything.

"Don't think. Don't wonder. Just agree."

Her mouth opened. Then shut. She hadn't a clue what to say.

"Annabel."

"Yes," she whispered.

"What time will you be home tomorrow night?"

"Um...midnight." He didn't move his finger while she answered, and the sensation of her lips moving over his skin started her heating up.

"I'll be at your house at midnight. Wear whatever mood you're in."

Her head started spinning. She was barely able to grasp any of this. Wear her mood? "What do you mean?"

"Surprise me, Annabel."

"Oh." She still whispered, unable to produce tone, breathing high and fast, color blooming in her cheeks. "Yes. Okay."

"Good." His voice dropped; he moved his finger gently back and forth on her mouth, as if he were a hypnotist, luring her into a trance. "I think I'll be able to surprise you, too."

3

To: John Brightman
From: Quinn Garrett
Date: December 19
Subject: Annabel

John, I looked up your sister. It was great to see her, we had breakfast yesterday morning. She does seem very work focused, but aside from that, she's obviously healthy and sane, so I wouldn't worry too much. I'll see if I can drag her away for some fun while I'm here. Maybe something more sophisticated than stealing her Barbie's underwear and outfitting her hamsters in it.

I'm hoping she's forgotten that incident.

Quinn

To: Quinn Garrett
From: John Brightman
Date: December 19
Subject: Re: Annabel

Ralph, the panty-wearing hamster! As I recall Annabel was not amused. Didn't she stop speaking to us for two days? I'd forgotten she even had Barbie, I'm not sure she ever really played with it. But bring the panty episode up when you see her next. If she doesn't laugh now, I really will worry.

Thanks for the report. If business keeps you there over Christmas, see if you can tempt her into some celebration. You remember what a big deal Christmas was to my parents. I hate thinking of her holed up alone in her house every year.

(For some reason, she accuses me of being a mother hen. Can you, ahem, imagine why she'd think such a thing?)

John

QUINN PULLED his car close to the curb opposite Annabel's house, lifted the vase of red, pink, white and yellow roses from the seat next to him, and emerged into the cold air, the smell of coming snow mingling with the delicate floral scent.

He'd called earlier to make sure Annabel would be out when he delivered the flowers. He wanted the chance to speak with her assistant, Stefanie, in person, get a better sense of what Annabel was about, how others perceived her, before he went too far with John's "rescue" idea. After all, John lived on the other side of the country. How much could he really know about Annabel's life and what she needed? On the other hand, he was her brother, and from what Quinn could tell, they were fairly close siblings.

Either way, he wanted to find out as much about her as possible. And if that made him sound slightly obsessed, so be it. The depth of his fascination defied logic.

She reminded him of her father, a big, no-nonsense, military man with a larger-than-life personality, impossible to please, measuring out compliments and love to his children in sparing doses so as not to spoil them. At thirteen, Annabel had had a tempestuous relationship with him, two kindred spirits butting heads, though she'd had plenty of her mother's softer side, too. Now, if John were to be believed, it seemed her father's genes had won out.

There were other feelings, too, beyond fascination. Feelings that had invaded him in force when she opened the door the other night and he got his first close-up look at his memorized brown-eyed, brunette, apple-cheeked adolescent image of her grown taller, softened and filled out here, slimmed and carved in there. An instant recognition, a year's worth of good memories and brotherly affection had swarmed him. Add to that, entirely in the present, a wave of sexual attraction so strong he could barely keep from making a move on her right there.

He'd gone home that night and lain in bed, unable to sleep thanks to the fantasies his mind would not stop inventing. And the thought had come to him with the calm certainty that thoughts often came to him—as if he could predict his own future, or as if he'd already lived his life and was simply remembering—that he would experience the explosive passion of their coming together in more than just fantasy. Soon.

He climbed the steps to her front door, rang the bell and waited, glancing around at the attractive rows of bungalows and stone houses that varied by differing roof and trim colors. A nice middle-class family neighborhood. Interesting that she hadn't chosen to live in a trendy downtown area, or in the more sophisticated neighborhoods north of the city where her cousin lived.

Money had not been a problem in her childhood, as it had been chronically in his.

So what did she hunger for? Fame? Recognition? Approval? Money entirely her own? What drove her? Her father's barely concealed disdain for women aspiring to or attaining high places? Quinn would find out. It was no accident that he'd mentioned the biography of Napoleon at breakfast the previous morning. He'd sensed that same chronic restlessness in her, a restlessness that would doom her to a lifelong search, unless she learned to find peace in the here and now. Maybe that peace was what John wanted for his sister.

The arched wooden door opened slowly to reveal a thin, pale young woman with fine, shoulder-length blond hair, who looked as if she hadn't slept in a week. He'd expected Stefanie to be a carbon copy of Annabel, at least in energy and spirit.

"Stefanie?"

"Yes." She extended a small, cool hand that felt as if it might break in his grasp. "Hello, Mr. Garrett."

"Quinn, please."

"Quinn. It's nice to meet you. What beautiful roses. Come on in."

He followed her into the familiar living room, tastefully if sparsely decorated in muted colors, lacking life and energy without its owner there, caught bundled in pajamas and an old robe by an unexpected nocturnal visitor. He'd sensed Annabel's discomfort, her longing to be as sleekly and confidently put together as she'd been the next morning at breakfast. Little did she know how that first rumpled sight of her had fueled his dreams that night.

"Would you like to put the roses in Annabel's office?" Stefanie glanced at him, then away. There was something furtive about her, something self-protective; he couldn't quite grasp what it was yet. Was she uneasy around him? Anxious about letting him in without Annabel here? Or simply nervous by nature?

"That would be fine."

She led him through the dining room and around the corner, into a room astoundingly devoid of color and personality. How could someone as colorful as Annabel—he'd seen her only in red so far—surround herself with so much bland professionalism?

He put the flowers on her neatly organized desk and stepped back next to Stefanie to consider them. The effect of the brilliant splash in the dull room was nearly violent. "I guess you can't miss them."

Stefanie laughed. "I offered to decorate for the holidays, but she refused."

"Really."

Stefanie shrugged, obviously unwilling to offer up the opinion of her boss he was after.

"Why do you think that is?"

"Oh. Well, she's so busy. And the holidays are always so busy. And I guess…she's…" Stephanie's frantic gestures subsided as she seemed to run out of possible explanations. Or politically correct ones.

"Busy?"

"Yes." Stefanie laughed abruptly. "Things might be going well, but they could be going better."

He narrowed his eyes. "Is that what she says?"

"It's her motto, she had me tape it to my computer." Stefanie turned to walk into a room across the tiny hall. "Here."

Quinn followed and nodded at the black-lettered sign adorning one of Holocorp's HC-2s. More, more, better, better…as he feared. "I take it that wouldn't have been your decorating choice?"

"Oh, I don't mind. It's a good motto. She certainly puts it into practice. I swear she never takes a day off. Never even an hour. When I leave every day I get the feeling she's not even close to winding down. She's amazing."

Not quite the word he'd use. He pointed to the tiny tree on Stefanie's desk, lights blinking on and off, tiny plastic presents under the green fake-needled branches. "Nice touch."

Stefanie blushed, bringing welcome color into her pretty face. "Silly, I suppose, but I need something to remind me of Christmas. *I* love this time of year."

She emphasized "I" just enough to send the message that Annabel didn't. "Bob Cratchit working for Scrooge?"

"Oh, no, she's not bad. I like her a lot—she's a great person." Stefanie stooped to turn up a space heater blasting away in the already-warm room, and put her hand protectively on her abdomen. "Sorry, but I can't stay warm in this house."

"Why don't you ask Annabel to turn up the heat?"

"She teases me all the time how cold is good for me. I finally just bought a heater."

Quinn frowned. First rule of good management, whenever you can, keep your employees happy in whatever ways you can. The little things mattered. "I see."

"I don't want you to think it's a problem." Stefanie stared at him anxiously. "It's definitely not a problem."

Quinn forced a smile. It was a problem. One so easily resolved. "How long have you been working for Annabel?"

"Since she started Chefs Tonight, a year or so ago."

"What did you do before that?"

"Oh, well, I was a hostess at a couple of restaurants, a waitress. Seems I'm always involved with food in some way. But I like working here."

"You don't get lonely stuck in a back room all day?"

"No, Annabel's here a lot, and she has really sweet neighbors on both sides, Kathy across the street—she runs a day care—and Chris to the north, we have lunch sometimes. This is a great block. The kids are out playing all summer long and after school, it's very cheerful."

"So Annabel is close to her neighbors."

"Oh. Well, not exactly. But I've gotten to know them and they're great people. See, Annabel is so busy she doesn't really have time for friends. There's her brother, John, who you know, I guess, and then once in a while there's a new guy who calls for a while until she breaks it off…*she* always breaks it off." Stefanie rolled her eyes. "Trail of broken hearts around the city. Maybe you'll have better luck."

Quinn chuckled, filing the information away. Was Annabel so driven she couldn't fall in love? Too blind to see the opportunities? Or did she deliberately choose men who couldn't touch her and interfere with her work? "I'm an old friend of the family."

"Oh. I'm sorry! I didn't mean... I mean, I know she knew you before, but then the roses today…I thought…" She winced and put her finger to her head as if it were the barrel of a gun. "Shut up, Stefanie."

"A natural assumption." He was definitely in luck—Stefanie was a talker. "What did Annabel do before this?"

"She had another business. With…a friend." Stefanie's expression closed down. She put her hand again to her abdomen, rubbed briefly and stifled a yawn.

"Something went wrong." He spoke gently, to encourage her confidence.

"Oh, well, they wanted different things, I guess. Tanya has a shop in Hartland, Tanya's Good Taste. Candy and all kinds of gourmet foods. She's doing really well. But I probably shouldn't be telling you any of this. You should probably ask Annabel." Stefanie moved around to sit heavily at her desk, as if her legs wouldn't hold her up anymore.

"Okay." Quinn's instinct sharpened. He walked to the back window, gazed out at the tiny backyard, the two-car garage easily taking up half. Then he turned his head so he could speak softly and Stefanie could still hear him. His next move was unorthodox, but he needed to see her reaction. "When are you due?"

An enormous gasp came from behind the desk. "Oh, my gosh. How did you know?"

He turned and smiled. "Congratulations."

"Did Annabel tell you? Does she know?" A worried frown creased her forehead, and she clutched her stomach as if the idea of Annabel finding out made her violently ill.

He shook his head. As he suspected. "If you haven't told her, she probably doesn't know."

"I haven't told her." She stared at her hands, fidgeting in her lap. "See, I'm due July Fourth, and with Memorial Day and the holiday, that's a busy time for us, and I'm not sure…I mean I'm afraid…"

Quinn's lips tightened. "She can't fire you."

"Oh, I know. But…well, I don't know how she'll manage. She once said she was glad I wasn't planning to have children. I mean that's what I told her in the interview and it was true then, but this happened by accident and Frank and I found we really want this baby, so here I am. And if I want to ask for maternity leave…well, it's a mess." She bit her lip. "I shouldn't even be telling you all this."

"It won't go further than me. But you need to tell Annabel."

"I know, I know." Stefanie lifted one hand and let it drop hopelessly in her lap. "I just dread it."

"Tell you what." He approached her desk and leaned his hands on its edge. "Wait until after the first of the year."

She lifted her head. "Why then?"

He winked. "I have a few reasons, fairly personal."

"Oh." An enormous grin lit up her tired face. "So maybe I wasn't so wrong about the roses?"

"Possibly not." He smiled. He liked Stefanie. And she'd told him enough to confirm what John had said, and convince him that Annabel could use a little nudge in a calmer direction. "Tell me something, Stefanie."

"Yes?"

"Does Annabel have anything important scheduled tomorrow, anything she can't miss?"

Stefanie chuckled and flipped a page of the calendar on her desk, drew her finger down the neatly made entries. "She would undoubtedly disagree, but from what I can see, no, nothing. Ted's doing the Henkels, no parties for once."

"Excellent."

"So…" Stefanie looked up slyly. "Is it fair to assume Ms. Brightman won't be in the office tomorrow?"

"I think that's a very fair assumption."

"Good."

"You approve?"

"Definitely." Stefanie leaned toward him over her desk and glanced into the hall as if she was afraid someone would overhear her next words. "Call me crazy, call me hormonal, call me whatever you want…but I think this time Annabel's met her match."

ANNABEL BOLTED from her garage to the back door, racing the icy winds whipping down her driveway, which not only wanted to remove any and all moisture from her exposed skin, but also made her breath jump back down her throat and huddle there for warmth. The cold front had arrived right on schedule; the windchill must be down in negative Fahrenheit territory.

Brrr.

She fumbled with her keys, reluctantly snatching one sheepskin mitten from her hand so her fingers could select the proper one more easily. *Hurry, hurry.* Eleven-thirty—she only had half an hour to shower and dress, to wear whatever mood she was in.

What mood was she in? Right now, jittery and frantic. She felt in her bones that Quinn would be precisely on time.

But jittery and frantic would not make an attractive presentation.

At all.

She jammed the key in the lock, twisted, turned and burst through the door. Leaped up the back stairs and smacked her keys onto the tiny phone nook cut into the wall, then dashed into her office, already shrugging out of her parka, to hang—

What was this?

She flicked on the light, pushed her thoroughly blown hair off her face and stared. The most amazing assortment of roses. Yellow, pink, white, red, oh, my goodness. Hand to her chest, she moved toward the card, daring it to be signed by who she *so* wanted it to be signed by.

Not a grateful client. Not a family member wishing her well. Not a friend sending joys of the season. Not that any of those had ever happened.

But, please, one sexually amazing corporate giant? Maybe a little smitten with her? Enchanted at the very least? Maybe saying as much? Or how he could not *wait* to see her tonight?

Maybe?

She plucked the envelope from the plastic-pronged holder and pulled out the card, parka still dangling off one arm. Black ink. Strong masculine handwriting.

To Annabel. So you can stop and smell them. Quinn.

Huh?

Damn and scowling disappointment. *So you can stop and smell them?* For crying out loud, he sounded like her brother.

What was with men, particularly high-powered men? They couldn't handle women who wanted to get places. Just like her father, who made her mom give up a promising career as a lawyer to be his full-time wife. Bet Quinn never told his male colleagues to take it easy. Bet he was never concerned about their mental health or their personal development. But oh, no! Women shouldn't hurt their delicate little selves shooting for anything like the big time.

God forbid. After all, what would men have to lord over them if women made success look as good as they did?

She jerked the second half of her coat off and hung it in the closet at the back of the room. Whether they liked it or not, she'd been born to take her place among the leaders. When other girls had been playing dress-up or planning trips to the shopping mall, she'd been playing Risk, plotting to take over the world. While other girls had batted their eyes and played stupid, sat on the sidelines and cheered, Annabel had excelled at her studies with pride, taken the field and played ferociously.

The closet door swung under the force of her shove, hit the jamb with a satisfying thud, then bounced back open slightly. She took a deep breath and turned to face the flowers again. They were beautiful. And unless she wanted to "wear her mood" and show up dressed for heavy combat, she'd better calm down.

Granted, maybe, possibly, yes, okay, she had a teeny-weeny chip on her shoulder. Her father had made it clear that women weren't ever going to take the place of men on the battlefield of life, and that those who tried somehow betrayed their gender. He'd encouraged her brother, applauded his achievements, and while Annabel was his special little girl and always would be, she got the sense that when John had chosen teaching instead of big business, he'd left a hole Dad never bothered hoping Annabel could fill. Certainly not with something as girly as food service.

Was that what drove her? Partly, sure, that—and

her own Dad-inherited need to do things in a big way.
But the drive certainly fueled her irritation at the message on the flowers, which Quinn had bought to be
supportive and thoughtful, so she should chill the heck
out and…she glanced at her watch…yikes! Get
dressed!

She took the stairs two at a time, launched herself
into her room and came to a stop in front of the closet.
All day she'd been distracted by thoughts of this date—
what would they do? what would she wear? where
would they go? would they…*mmm*…or not?—and finally decided to take Quinn at his word, wait to see what
mood she was in and dress accordingly.

Now she wished she'd planned ahead, her usual
strategy.

So…

Would they be going out? Staying in? There wasn't
much open now. Milwaukee was hardly the city that
never slept. If they went out, she'd need something
warm to combat the icy temperatures. But if they stayed
in…she could get away with next-to-nothing.

Gulp.

Could she open the door to him in next-to-nothing?

Her stomach growled. She was starving, so she hoped
the evening involved food, though if they stayed here,
she had almost nothing to offer him, which meant—

Okay, Annabel, focus. Clothes first, the evening
would decide itself.

She scanned the contents of her closet and glanced
at her watch. Twenty minutes. Ack!

Pants? A Dress? Skirt?

Deep breath. *Calm down.* If she dressed her mood

now, she'd have to wear something so full of static she'd crackle if anyone went near her.

First she needed to decide her mood. Something besides frazzled. She took more deep breaths, then deeper ones, closed her eyes, imagined seeing Quinn—how would she feel? Not quite daring. Not quite demure. Available, but not easy. Calm, confident, in control.

She opened her eyes and approached her closet again. She slid a hand between a black rayon blouse and white silk and encountered something exquisitely soft. Cashmere. Annabel drew the top out and smiled. Apricot-colored cashmere, wide neck, nearly off the shoulder, fairly tight fit.

Pair it with a slit-to-heaven, knee-length black wool skirt. Seductive without being obviously so, good to go out, good to stay in.

Yes.

She shed her sensible slim-fitting black gabardine pants and acrylic knit sweater, her skin and nerves enjoying the air and freedom. Stepped out of her Victoria's Secret cotton panties, unhooked and pulled off her underwire bra, raced to the shower to soap off the kitchen smells, and came back into her room, too nervous to glance at the clock. Calm? Did she say she wanted to be calm?

Focus.

Underwear: black lace micro-bikini. Matching push-up bra. Sheer black thigh-high stockings.

Makeup: eyeliner, mascara, concealer, blush, the barest smear of deep rosy apricot color on her lips.

Before she put the skirt and top on, she stole to the mirror to check herself out. Would he see her this way tonight? Dressed only in black lace and nylon? Would he want to?

Oh, she hoped so. She very, very much hoped so. She looked good, her body slender, firm and strong. And suddenly she felt good, the way she looked, the way she wanted to appear—calm, confident and sexual.

A chuckle escaped her. He'd said to dress her mood. Well, this was pretty much it.

As if he'd heard her thoughts, someone she assumed was Quinn chose that exact moment to ring her front doorbell.

Annabel started and glanced at her clock.

Midnight. On the dot.

4

So.

Annabel let out a two-second burst of nervous laughter. Quinn Garrett was waiting outside on her front steps and all she had on were bare coverings of lace and nylon.

She glanced at the apricot sweater and black skirt lying on the cherry rocking chair in her room, and again at herself in the mirror. Hadn't he said to surprise him? Hadn't she just said she looked and felt strong and confident?

Yes, but there was a difference between feeling strong and confident alone in her bedroom and answering the door to someone she didn't know that well wearing only underwear.

The bell rang again; Annabel snatched up the sweater and dragged it on, stepped into the skirt and ran downstairs zipping it up behind her. She'd certainly like him to see her in sexy underwear—and less—but maybe before the first date even began was pushing it. Second date? She'd have to see. Assuming he was interested in her, and not just acting on orders from her brother, John. Though she couldn't imagine this man acting on orders from anyone but himself.

She ran through the still-dark living room, flipped on the outside light, yanked open the outer door and padded into the foyer, the brick-colored tile chilling her stockinged feet as she opened the front door to Quinn.

"Hello." She smiled breathlessly. He was stunning in his long black wool coat and white silk scarf. Elegant like Pierce Brosnan, primal like Russell Crowe, his breath emerging white and steady in the icy air. "Sorry to make you wait, you caught me half-dressed."

"What a shame."

She wasn't sure how to take that, and his faintly amused expression didn't help at all, so she stepped back and gestured him inside. "Come in."

He preceded her into her unlit living room. For a guilty moment she lingered behind him, enjoying his tall, black, broad-shouldered presence. She'd brought a few men home in her time, but none of them had filled the place the way this one did. Was his aura really that powerful or was her fascination simply feeding it? Or both?

The tall, black, broad-shouldered shape turned, making Annabel aware that gawking at him in the darkness was a tad on the weird side.

"Sorry for the mole atmosphere." She hurried to turn on the floor lamp beside the couch. "I had to rush after I got home—oh, and thank you so much for the flowers."

"You're welcome."

She turned on another lamp, feeling as if she should say something more, maybe something about the smell-the-roses note, but given how it had hit her the wrong way, she couldn't risk sounding snarky. "They're beautiful."

"I'm glad you like them." He put his hands on his hips, pushing back the edges of his coat, and studied her, again giving her the feeling he was dissecting her brain, understanding everything she wasn't saying about the note. How did he do that?

"I want you to enjoy them."

"Oh, I will." Annabel smiled agreeably. He was so hard to read. He wanted her to enjoy them, yes, but they symbolized more than that. An implicit criticism of her lifestyle and ambition. Something her father would have done, only not so subtly.

His eyes traveled over her outfit; his lips hinted at a smile without giving one.

"So your clothes are telling me you're in the mood to do just about anything."

She nodded, wondering what he'd have done if she'd opened the door in black lace. Though from what she could see of his dark trousers and what looked like a suit jacket, he was feeling too formal to jump her.

Darn.

"Yes, I'm up for anything."

"Have you eaten?"

"No. Have you?"

He shook his head, reached into his coat pocket and produced a small package wrapped in tissue and a plastic bag. "I found this at an antique shop downtown today."

She nodded politely, confused by the non sequitur, and watched him unwrap an exquisite miniature dresser, barely five inches high, that looked as if it belonged in an extremely fancy dollhouse, the kind she had been in awe of as a child, not that she'd played with dolls that much, but just to have something so lovely in her room.

"It's beautiful." She approached and touched the tiny thing reverently. Tortoiseshell, it looked like, with ornate brass overlay. Three drawers, complete with tiny handles and miniature brass keyholes. Stunning and no doubt valuable. "Are you a collector?"

"It's for you."

Annabel jerked her head up to meet his dark eyes; her mouth opened, then shut. The combination of surprise and the shock of attraction left her brainpower nearly blacking out. "But…I mean you've already…the flowers…"

"It's a game."

She glanced down at the tiny piece of furniture. "A game."

"It came with three keys, one for each drawer." He rummaged in the plastic bag and came up with a miniature Ziploc bag containing three of the tiniest brass keys she'd ever seen. "Would you like to play?"

"How?"

"Pick a key. Each drawer has an idea for how we spend the evening. Whichever your key opens, that's what we do."

She laughed, surprised Quinn Garrett had a whimsical side. She would have thought he was so tightly controlled, he'd never leave their plans up to the roll of a dice—or in this case the turn of a key. The guys she dated were generally uncomplicated, what-you-see-is-what-you-get. Quinn seemed anything but. "What are my choices?"

"Do you have to know?"

"Yes." She lifted her chin. "I'm a control freak. I have to know."

He appeared to be thinking that over, but she'd bet it wasn't exactly news. "You never give up control?"

"Never."

"Hmm." He emptied the tiny keys from the bag into

his large palm, where they looked even tinier. "Then we have a problem."

"Why's that?"

He lifted his head. "I don't either."

Annabel stared up at his impassive face, trying to get a handle on what had suddenly flared between them, other than the obvious chemistry. For some reason she got an immediate picture of herself straddling him, making him beg for the release only she could give him.

Mmm, twisted. Let him mind-read *that*.

Quinn did smile then, a slow spreading of those fabulous lips, though not far, as if the mechanism were rusted. "A challenge for both of us."

Heat found her face. Rather than mind reading, maybe he'd been thinking the same kind of thoughts about her that she'd been thinking about him all on his own. She liked that idea.

"So what are my choices?"

He arranged the three keys between his thumb and index finger so they stuck up like a tiny fan. "A private screening of *The Thomas Crown Affair* at the Rosebud Cinema."

"Ooh. Yes?"

"A private after-hours dinner at Sanford Restaurant."

"Mmm. And?"

"A private evening." His voice dropped. "In your bedroom. Or in mine."

Annabel drew in a breath so long she wasn't sure it would ever stop. "Oh, my."

He took a step closer. She could feel his warmth radiating across the few inches left separating them. *Oh, my.*

"Choose a key, Annabel."

"I'd rather just pick an evening?"

"Which one?"

"The third." She was whispering, nearly faint with excitement. "Definitely."

He shook his head and held up the miniature keys. "Choose."

Annabel bit her lip, examining the tiny strips of brass as if one of them might have "all-night sexathon" engraved on it. Then her eyes slipped upward, landed on his, and lust ran so hot through her she could barely stand it. "Quinn…"

"Which key?"

She forced her eyes back down and, with embarrassingly shaky fingers, selected the one in the middle. He seemed as cool and collected as ever, damn him, while she was practically climaxing just thinking about being with him. "This one."

He handed her the miniature key and her embarrassingly shaky fingers got even more embarrassing as she tried to fit the metal sliver into the first lock.

"Relax." He drew warm fingers over the skin of her shoulder exposed by her sweater's wide neckline, slid them to the back of her neck and massaged lightly.

"Touching me is not going to make me relax."

"No?"

"No." She was whispering again. His fingers were strong and skillful and incredibly arousing.

The key didn't work in the first drawer. She took a breath, pressing back against his fingers, and moved it to the second. He walked around behind her, spread his hands on her shoulders and made glorious circles of

pressure with his thumbs in the middle of her back
where all her tension collected.

"Ohh, that's heaven." She tipped her head to one
side, feeling the length of her neck sensitive and exposed when gravity swept her hair aside. Her head
dropped back, nearly to his chest, and she closed her
eyes. His breath caught briefly; his fingers lost their
rhythm, then found it again. Annabel lifted her head, trying not to smile and give away her satisfaction. Maybe
not so cool and collected?

The second drawer didn't open, either. She fit the key
into the third lock, twisted, opened it, heart pounding,
and pulled out paper folded into an impossibly tiny origami bird. "Did you do this?"

"Yes."

He pulled her back against him briefly, a moment of
heavenly contact with his strong, warm body, then let
her go and watched her unfold the creases with her yes,
okay, by now ridiculously shaky hands.

Dinner at Sanford's.

For a moment she stared at the words, as if her brain
was so primed to see "your place or mine" that it refused
to accept anything else.

Damn.

"Excellent."

She turned to face him and held up the paper. "This
is the one you wanted?"

He lifted an eyebrow. "One appetite at a time."

"Do I get to open the others after dinner?"

He folded his arms like a stern father. "No."

Annabel laughed in spite of her disappointment.
Okay, regroup. Yes, she was starving. And Sanford Res-

taurant arguably served the best food in town. Plus, mmm, they could still find their way to his place or hers later on.

She gave herself a mental smack. And when was she planning to sleep? Tomorrow was another day, she had calls to make, people she had to—

"I'll tell you a secret."

Annabel blinked and brought herself back. "What's that?"

He leaned down next to her ear, making her skin buzz, making her want to turn her head just a few degrees and grab his lips in the sexiest kiss she could give him.

"All the drawers had the same option."

"What?" She stopped wanting to kiss him, and glared accusingly instead. "You're kidding."

"Dead serious. You can have the other two keys if you want to check."

"But that's not fair."

"Did I say it was fair?"

"You led me on."

"Yes."

"You manipulated me."

"Yes. And?"

"So, that's…well, it's dishonest. And creepy."

"Maybe." He grinned then, the rare stunning smile that changed his whole face and reminded her so much of the boy she used to know.

"But Annabel, wasn't it fun?"

ANNABEL LET her head loll back on the seat of Quinn's rented Lexus speeding west on I 94 toward her house, and closed her eyes, not tired at all but wanting to savor and relive the evening. Oh, what a good meal. Champagne to start, then a salad of grilled shrimp with grapefruit vinaigrette, seafood cassoulet, lavender honey-roasted suckling pig and a to-die-for bittersweet chocolate tart. The chef was an artist. She'd love to sneak some of those recipes into her repertoire. One of these days she'd have to go suckling-pig shopping and experiment.

What it had cost Quinn to have the chef stay this late and keep the restaurant open for the two of them, even with a skeleton staff, she didn't want to know, but it had been fabulous. Luxurious, leisurely and so-o-o intimate. One of these nights she'd have to cook for Quinn herself—at her own private restaurant.

Right now, though, she was full, jazzed, happy, pleasantly tipsy and mildly infatuated. These were good things. Now she could go home, get four or five hours of sleep and start her day tomorrow with the promise of seeing more of Quinn in the near future. Maybe even tomorrow night if he was free and willing.

He'd been easy to talk to, not so much the man of few words he'd been in her apartment. After a few awkward beginnings, a few obviously polite questions, they'd begun to chat more naturally—of course the wine had helped that along. And while he was still a private person, and had this way of directing questions back so the conversation always seemed to center on her, they'd brought up some wonderful memories, things she hadn't thought of in years. Like the time he and John stayed out past curfew and had to sneak inside through her bedroom window because her furious father had locked them out. And the time he and John put Barbie's underwear on her hamster and she'd been so livid she hadn't spoken to them for days.

Of course tonight, picturing poor little Ralph frantic in pink nylon practically made her spit out her champagne laughing.

One memory, however, had intruded totally unexpectedly while they reminisced about her parents' annual Christmas party, startling Annabel into trailing off mid-sentence. Immediately, Quinn had given her that I'm-reading-your-mind look, but though he might see she was rattled, even he couldn't possibly guess why. Or so she'd like to think.

This Christmas memory she hadn't shared at the restaurant. It seemed impossible she could have forgotten the episode in the first place, even more impossible that Quinn coming back into her life hadn't triggered it sooner. And teenage-foolishly, she had to wonder if he ever thought of it after he went back home that year, or if seeing her again now had made him remember.

It had been a few days before Christmas; her mother and father usually had their party on the twenty-first or twenty-second. They'd decorated the house to the nines as usual, red-bowed garlands climbing up the front banister, a candle in every window, the huge stuffed Santa doll her grandmother made, Advent calendars, the tree of course, variously framed or displayed dreadful holiday art projects she and John had made over the years, and always mistletoe in the front foyer where her parents stood, to greet their arriving guests and again to hand out gifts to those departing—popcorn balls wrapped in red cellophane for the children and sprays decorated with frosted pinecones and velvet ribbon for the grown-ups.

That year, the year Quinn lived with them, the last guests had just gone out into dark December clutching their sprays, Christmas greetings and good-nights floating after them on the icy air.

Her parents had closed the massive arched front door for the last time, sighed in satisfaction, smiled at each other with love, and had gone arm in arm to the kitchen to supervise putting the chaos back in order. Annabel had snuck into the deserted foyer to snitch ribbon candy from the dish by the door, figuratively drunk with sugar, the Christmas spirit and the aura of joyful companionship still cozying the house. She'd been singing one of the carols her father led the guests in during the party, one of her favorites, "It Came Upon The Midnight Clear," when Quinn had spoken suddenly behind her in his deep scratchy teenage voice and nearly scared her to death.

"You sing well."

She'd turned to find him staring at her and at her crimson velvet party dress in a way that made her wish fervently he hadn't caught her holding something as childish as Christmas candy.

"Thanks."

She'd stared back at him, unable to understand what she saw in his eyes, noticing not for the first time how handsome he was in his gray-and-blue sweater, the grown-up bulge of a dark necktie at his throat.

And during that strange combination of tense and natural, staring at each other with the atmosphere stretched so thin time must have stopped, the mistletoe had made a little rustling sound and fallen onto the floor between them.

Quinn had picked up the sprig calmly, as he did most things, as if he wasn't surprised in the least that it had been hanging up and now suddenly it wasn't. He'd taken the few steps toward her and held the tiny branch over her head.

She could imagine what she'd looked like, eyes the size of walnuts, slack jawed, probably not even breathing. She certainly remembered what she'd been thinking.

And then he'd said, "If you were older, I'd kiss you," laid the mistletoe on the table next to the ribbon candy and bowl of popcorn balls and walked upstairs without looking back.

She'd barely slept that night, reliving the moment over and over, hugging close the thrill each replay brought. By morning, reality intruded, she'd been so shy and unsure of herself, so full of the many emotions that scared and confused her, that she'd barely even glanced at him. For his part, he was back to his old self, a second big brother, and hadn't come near her in that intimate, private way, that day or again. Eventually she convinced herself he'd just been teasing and had gotten over it. For the most part.

"Tired?"

Annabel opened her eyes and turned her head toward him without lifting it from the seat. He was driving with one hand, glancing between her and the road.

"A little." Not at *all*. The evening had been so perfect she could make like Eliza Doolittle in *My Fair Lady* and dance all night. But how else to explain her long reverie? *I was actually thinking about the one time you nearly kissed me and was hoping you'd think I was plenty old enough tonight.* "Are *you* tired?"

"I seldom am. And never in the company of a woman who fires me up the way you do."

"I fire you up?"

"Absolutely."

She blinked innocently, holding back a smile. "What, like, spiritually, you mean?"

He sent over a slow, lazy-eyed glance that instantly got rid of her need to giggle and replaced it with a more mature need. "Not exactly."

Oh, my. Her sound of feigned disappointment made him smile. She loved that smile, a rare and sacred treat. She'd love even more to get him to do it often. "Intellectually then?"

The car approached the exit to Route 41 north…and passed it. He'd probably take the next exit, Hawley Road.

"Intellectually certainly."

Annabel shifted in her seat. Her coat fell open and exposed a length of her thigh, which she didn't bother to recover. Let him look. All the more fun built up for the next time they were together, if she got lucky and picked the right drawer…and got lucky.

"Hmm, so do I fire you up…some other way, maybe?"

He glanced over at her legs. *Just* to be cruel, she parted them, *just* a little bit.

"Definitely another way."

"How?"

"Sexually."

"Oh!" She gasped in pretended outrage and opened her legs a little more. "That's shocking."

"Isn't it."

"You shouldn't say things like that."

"No." He turned on his blinker and changed into the right lane. "I should say, 'Open your legs wider.'"

Annabel caught her breath. The command had come out calmly, naturally, as if he was asking her to roll down her window.

"Excuse me?"

He turned and looked her full in the eyes, then went back to driving.

A burn of lust started in her belly and down between the legs he wanted spread wider. She opened them more, her skirt riding up until the lace tops of her thigh-highs were exposed.

"How's that?" Her voice came out breathless and excited, because, she was damn breathless and damn excited—and getting more so every second.

"Wider."

She spread them all the way, coat open, skirt hiked up to her hips, black lace panties now visible in the dimly lit car.

He drew in a sharp breath, glancing back and forth from her wide-open legs to the road. "Put your seat back."

She fumbled for the handle, reclined the seat and lay there, turned-on out of her mind, waiting for what he'd do or say next, the car speeding down the highway, streetlights lighting and receding to darkness in a steady rhythm.

Quinn switched his left hand to the steering wheel, slipped his right hand out of its leather glove, and slid warm, slow, sure fingers up her thigh, over to the smooth sensitive center, and under her panties. Found her, wet, hot, aching for him, and began to stroke.

Clearly the man knew what he was doing.

She lifted her hips to his touch, wedged her knees and feet so she could thrust against him, and *oh* it was heaven. In a matter of one minute, she was so close to climaxing she could feel the sweat break on her body, the steady building of the sensation.

And the slowing of the car.

She opened dazed eyes to Quinn, who brought the car to an abrupt stop on the shoulder of the highway, just out of range of a streetlight, reached over her and opened the glove compartment.

Condoms.

Her breath went in and her arousal became so hot and needy she felt like a raging beast-woman. He wanted her here, barely a mile from her house, wanted her so badly he couldn't wait.

Neither could she.

He reached down and jerked back his seat, undid his pants, brought himself out, hard, proud and ready, and rolled on the condom. "Come here."

She shook her head, laughing, hot, breathless, already climbing over to him. "I can't believe we're going to do this. We could be arrested."

"We won't be arrested. Come here."

"I'm here, I'm here." She straddled him, pushing her panties aside. His arms came around her, lifted her hips up, then onto him and oh, the feel of him filling her up, she nearly came just from that, from his strength helping her move up and down over his cock, the whoosh of vehicles going by, shaking their car, and the frantic thrusting of their bodies reaching, reaching…

Her orgasm hit first. She cried out, thrashed on top

of him, trying to get it to stay, stay with her, keep him inside just like this, just like this…

"Annabel." He tensed, whispered her name again as he came, bringing her a new, shivery wave of excitement until slowly she came down.

Finished. Over. Oh, my word.

Quinn brushed a kiss over her cheek, clasped her hard to him, then let go. She climbed off, still breathing fast, body glowing, and collapsed in her seat. A nervous giggle bubbled up. "I can't believe we just did that."

"No?" He grabbed tissues from a box in the console between them, disposed of the condom and did up his pants, his movements brisk and efficient, not at all panicked or rushed, as if he did this all the—

Ew.

Annabel's thrill turned distinctly un-thrill-like. Did he? Go to strange towns, pick up women and screw them in his car on the way home? Was this not unbridled passion but just his fetish thing?

Double ew.

Quinn turned off the hazards, put the Lexus in gear, found a safe break in traffic and pulled the powerful car back out onto the highway.

Finished. Over. Oh, my word.

Annabel wrapped her coat around her. What had she done? What had—

Oh, come on. She wasn't going to play some bogus temporary insanity card—*Oh gee, what came over me?* She was an adult; she knew what she was doing. But he—

"What's wrong?" He reached over, took her hand and squeezed it gently.

"Nothing." She forced a smile, praying it was dark

enough in the car that he'd buy it. "That was really great."

"Tell me what's wrong."

"There's nothing to—"

"Annabel."

She sighed. "Yes."

"If we're going to see a lot of each other while I'm here, and I hope we are, you need to be honest with me or we'll poison whatever we're starting."

Annabel swallowed hard. She did not like being spoken to like a petulant child. Even if, yes, okay, she just happened to be acting like one. Damn him, he was right.

"I was just wondering if roadside sex is something you enjoy." She froze herself off. How did you politely ask someone about their sexual habits?

"Didn't I seem to be enjoying it?"

"I mean…frequently."

He chuckled, loosened his grip on her hand and changed to stroking her palm and the undersides of her fingers. The gesture felt warm and affectionate and nothing like what she imagined a fetishist would do. "The last time I had sex in a car I was barely old enough to drive it."

"Oh." She gave a silly giggle of relief and twined her fingers with his.

"What about you? Have those legs enticed many men into pulling over on Wisconsin's highways?"

"Oh, no." She tipped her head, narrowing her eyes. "Would it bother you if they had?"

"Absolutely." He spoke without hesitation, and her heart raced. "Same way it bothered you when you thought I might make this a habit."

"Yes."

"Then neither of us have to worry. This was something special for both of us. Ladies and gentlemen, the control freaks are tied at one apiece."

Annabel laughed and leaned her head back, feeling the contented glow of satiation returning. The evening was officially perfect. As much as she had wanted to take Quinn home and spend leisure time in bed, the truth was she didn't operate well on less than four hours of sleep and the clock was ticking. She had plenty to do tomorrow and didn't want to be exhausted trying to accomplish it all.

The sign for the Hawley Road exit glowed green in his headlights…and past.

"Didn't you mean to take that exit?" He'd have to backtrack to her house now.

"No."

She frowned. "But if you take Sixty-eighth —"

"I'm not taking Sixty-eighth."

"What?"

"I said I'm not taking Sixty-eighth."

"Uh. Qui-i-inn?"

"Ye-e-es?"

"Are you planning to take me home?"

He squeezed her hand again and let it go, turned and winked a wink that made her insides go a little nuts.

"No, Annabel, I'm not."

5

ANNABEL DRAGGED herself awake in the gloriously soft, warm unfamiliar bed at the Riverside B and B in Hartland.

Time. What time was it? It felt late. Light was creeping in around the blinds, but the alarm hadn't gone off yet. She turned and blinked at the clock, trying to get her eyes to focus...

Nine o'clock. *Nine!* She'd set the alarm for seven, what the—

She bolted upright, grabbed the clock and pushed the button to check the alarm setting.

Noon?

She couldn't possibly have screwed up. She'd set it last night for seven, turned it on, tested it. What could—

Huh? A note lay on the beautiful Shaker-style bedside table, between the rose-shaded lamp and the tissues in a fancy black lacquer box. A note on ivory paper with embossed initials "QG" in a bold navy font.

Sleep well, my beauty. Quinn

What? That hadn't been there when she—

Slowly Annabel's groggy brain caught up to what had happened. Quinn had happened. Again. He must have snuck in after she'd gone to sleep, and instead of having wild sex with her again, which was why she left the damn door unlocked in the first place, he'd changed the alarm and left the note.

Sleep well, my beauty? As in, until Prince Charming awakens her with a kiss and rescues her from her life?

Ohhhh, she was *so* going to have a little talk with Mr. Puppeteer. Last night was bad enough, bringing her to this place where he'd already reserved rooms for them, surprise, surprise—not. And yes, okay, she was sort of disappointed at the plural rooms, but then she could never sleep with another body taking up space in bed anyway. Maybe he was like that, too. Or maybe he had his public reputation to uphold, whatever.

He'd certainly been secretive and distant in the car last night, not telling her where they were going until they arrived, not telling her why he'd brought her here for the night. What was the point driving half an hour out of the way to spend one night and head back the next morning? Especially if they weren't even sharing rooms? Plus, it had started snowing on the drive over, coming down heavily by the time they pulled into the huge colonial's long driveway. Great. A big storm was all she needed. Good thing she wasn't due at a client's this morning. Or all day for that matter. But she sure had plenty else to do.

She bounced out of the four-poster bed and padded over quaint rag rugs laid on dark-honey hardwood into the blue-and-white-tiled bathroom, and glanced out the blue-curtained windows at the snow *still* coming down, darn it. The shower came on cold with no signs of turning warm quickly, so she made use of the facilities while the water heated, still thinking about Quinn.

Like she'd stopped since he rang her doorbell three nights ago?

To tell the truth, his reticence the night before had felt a little strange after that incredible sex in the car. Once she'd given up trying to pry his agenda out of him—and why had she ever thought she'd be able to?—they'd mostly driven in silence, then checked in equally quietly downstairs, where the apple-cheeked middle-aged proprietress could not beam hard enough at Quinn. He'd seemed distracted, or maybe simply back to his usual controlled self. Of course she and Quinn had only just met again. She hadn't anticipated—or even wanted—smothering affection. But after that fabulous sex, she hadn't expected him to act like…

She stopped with one leg sticking into the tub and frowned. Actually, he was sort of acting like…her.

Her frown grew deeper. Wasn't this how she behaved around the men she slept with? Hadn't a few of them complained that she turned them off like an overprocessing blender when the sex was finished? Is this what they felt like? Sort of abandoned and maybe a little…used?

Hmm.

But then men were famous for rolling over and going to sleep afterward, while women equally famously wanted the snuggle thing to go on for all eternity. Annabel had always had more of a male attitude toward sex, that was all.

So why did this bother her now?

She rolled her eyes. She'd get over it. Meanwhile her foot was getting a nice shower and the rest of her was still out in the cold, so she'd probably be smart to stop standing on one leg like a dork and get herself clean.

Ten minutes later, she'd showered and made use of the high-quality toiletries provided by their hosts, wrapped herself in the sky-blue terry robe hanging on the door and barged back into the room, not wanting to think about having to wear a short skirt and tiny black flats out into the snow. *Brr.* Maybe she could—

Annabel stopped short. On her made-up bed, neatly laid out, were a pair of cozy-looking bright red tapered knit pants, delicate long underwear—silk?—a white sweatshirt decorated with a holly print down both sleeves and along the neck, snow boots, red suede mittens, and a red stocking cap that read Ho-ho-ho in green letters around the white brim.

And another blasted note.

Thought these might come in handy for our adventures today. Quinn.

Today? Adventures *today?* Not tonight after work? What was he smoking? And why hadn't she taken a clue from the alarm-clock adventure and locked the door while she was showering?

And…damn her for even thinking it, but why hadn't he tried to join her in the shower? Not that she had time, of course, silly thought. The only thing she wanted to do today was get back home and get busy.

She marched out into the hall and lifted her fist to knock on Quinn's door.

Of course Mr. Psychic opened it immediately and she nearly found herself knocking on his…on his…forehead and…um…

Oh, he looked *so* good. Hair damp and mussed from the shower, chamois shirt in a sophisticated olive-gray-blue plaid hanging open to show the smooth white tee hugging his chest, rugged olive-colored pants that perfectly matched the shirt—*he'd* known to pack an overnight bag, of course. Her fingers uncurled from knocking position and she had to pull her hand down to keep from smoothing the unruly hair off his forehead, just as an excuse to touch him, really, since the unrulies looked so sexy as is.

Wait. Ahem. Where was her outrage?

"Good morning, Annabel."

"Oh. Good morning." Hello? Outrage? She couldn't summon enough of it to launch into her planned attack. For some reason, the sight of him and the sound of his rich, deep voice saying her name made her feel ridiculously happy.

What was this?

"There's an outfit on my bed." She folded her arms across her chest before she realized her words made absolutely no sense—and knew he'd understand perfectly.

"Why aren't you wearing it?" He looked about to smile, as if he not only knew damn well why she wasn't wearing it, but also looked forward to the showdown, because he knew he'd win.

Not so fast, lover boy.

"I can't have adventures with you today. This is a workday for me."

"Oh?" He reached for the ties on her robe and drew her into the room.

"Quinn."

"Mmm?" His left hand went to the door and shoved to close it.

No. She shot out her arm and caught the edge behind her. "You kidnapped me, okay, but now it's time for me to get back on track."

"The fast track?"

"Damn straight."

"I see." He reached for her ties again; she backed against the door, grabbed the robe sash and knotted it firmly.

"Well, well." He held her defiant gaze, a slow, wicked gleam coming into his eyes that excited her and—strangely—unnerved her. "I sense a stalemate."

"Checkmate. Your loss."

"I wouldn't be too sure."

She pulled the lapels of her robe closer together, then hated herself for betraying her unease. But with that intense predatory stare, Quinn was making her feel as naked under her robe as...she was. "No?"

"No." He dropped to his knees, spread the edges of her robe below the knotted belt and pinned her hips back against the door with his large warm hands.

She gasped and reached down instinctively to cover herself.

"Don't move."

She put her hands back up and held still, barely registering the cool room air on her exposed sex before she felt Quinn's warm breath replacing it.

Oh, oh, my. She clutched her lapels tighter together, thickly swaddled above the waist and utterly vulnerable and open to him below.

"What a sight."

Annabel closed her eyes, experiencing a moment of strange shyness in spite of the reverence in his whisper. Since when had she been at all reticent about showing her body to a lover?

"Beautiful." He moved closer and blew gently, wide-mouthed, a hot steady stream that made Annabel lean her head back until it thudded to rest against the door.

"So tell me what happens if you don't accomplish today what you want to?" He whispered the words, then his mouth kissed her sex, a warm, lingering kiss.

Oh, she was so, so lost. "Um…I'll get…behind."

"Behind what?" His tongue found her, warm and wet, light strokes over her clitoris, then down lower, spreading and exploring, making her abdominal muscles contract and her hips push forward.

"My…schedule."

"I see." His mouth tightened over her clit; he sucked in a steady rhythm. Annabel lifted her head from the door, let it thud back, did it again, hot and restless, feeling the urgency of wanting to come, not wanting him to stop. Ever.

Except that he did. "So you might end up an entire day behind…what? Or whom?"

She swallowed, the sound loud in the room, silent except for her ragged breathing. This would not be a good time to bring up Adolph Fox's frozen entrées. "Behind in my goals."

"Ah." He moved forward and his tongue shot her to heaven again, all the more for the teasing pause that preceded it—a long, leisurely series of strokes before he— *no, no*—stopped again. "Your goals have a precise expiration date? If not accomplished by Tuesday the twenty-third of two-thousand-whatever they are no longer viable?"

She made a sound of frustration, wanting his tongue to stop talking and go back to making her nuts. "If I don't keep up the momentum…if I don't stay hungry…"

"Then what?"

"I'll…stop being hungry." She made herself sound

confident. She knew what she was talking about, no matter how he twisted it.

"So push the date of your success back one day and the balance of Annabel's universe is forever lost."

"Quinn." She gestured and let her hands drop, arousal beginning to fade into exasperation.

"I'm here."

"I'd love to spend the day with you, that's not the issue." She took hold of his wrists, intending to get him to release her. "I just need to get to work."

His wrists didn't budge. She might as well have been trying to dislodge burned caramel from a saucepan with Q-Tips.

"Let go of—"

He lunged forward again, pressed his mouth to her sex, tongue working in earnest.

Annabel cried out; her head hit the door again with a sharp crack. If there was pain, she didn't feel it. She was too swallowed up by the pleasure he was giving her.

Oh, oh, yes. She spread her legs wider, pushed her hips forward; his tongue left her clit, traveled down, then up inside her with thrusts that made her ache for the feel of his penis the same way.

"Quinn."

"Mmm?"

"On the bed."

"No time." Back to her clit, he worked it with utter confidence and a sense of purpose that sent her over the edge.

"Oh." The climax built then burned through. Her hands reached, trying to grasp hold of something on the smooth walls, head twisting side to side.

Then pulsing release, over and over…and Quinn's

tongue slowing to keep pace with her comedown, teasing her into aftershocks until she couldn't anymore.

His strong arms supported her undignified and limp slide into a languid, sated heap on the floor. She smiled and reached to touch his cheek, stroke his fine jaw. He turned and kissed her palm, helped her stand again, kissed her forehead and each temple, and...drew back. Left her standing there offering her mouth, feeling like a geek on a disaster prom date. Okay. No kissing. But didn't he at least want her to return the favor sexually? "What about you?"

He trailed gentle fingers down her shoulders, arms, over her wrists and pulled her hands into his. "Another time."

"Not now?" She moved closer, let her pelvis brush seductively across his erection.

"Believe me, I won't say no later. This morning I have other plans for us." He brought her hands to his lips and kissed them, one then the other. "But right now I want to know why spending one day with me would be such a terrible mistake, something you seem to think you'd regret for the rest of your life."

Annabel closed her eyes. Oh, jeez. Why did he have to put it that way? It made her sound so...foolish. And selfish. And misguided.

Which was exactly why he put it that way—so he could win. And worse, in her state of extreme...languor, shall we say...with his body and charisma and—maleness, damn it—exerting that incredible magnetic pull on her good sense, Annabel wanted him to win. And he knew that, too.

She opened her eyes to insist that she didn't buy tickets for anyone's guilt trips, but he put his hands to her face and gently laid his forehead to hers and the words died in a rush of lovely warmth.

She sighed. "No, I wouldn't regret it for the rest of my life. But—"

"Then we're on."

She didn't need to see his smug expression. She knew it was there. Knew he'd probably planned this whole discussion, probably her orgasm, too. He had her right where he planned her to be at exactly the time he intended.

And guess what? He was so damn good at it that she wanted to be here. Except she couldn't let him walk all over her without some conditions. "I need to be home by lunch."

"After."

"Before." She lifted her head and held his gaze, forcing hers to remain steady.

"Okay. Agreed."

"And my giving in does not hand you the right to trick me again. You might have won this time, but—"

"Annabel, I'll just have to ask you to trust me on something." He stepped away from her, put his hands on his hips and regarded her grimly. "You might not think so now, but believe it or not, this way we both win."

THE MINUTE the Lexus turned off Highway JK onto a long two-lane farm road, Annabel knew where Quinn was taking her.

"This is where Dad used to get our Christmas tree every year."

Quinn smiled, the smile that made her want to dance in delight—except the Lexus was a tad small for that.

He'd emerged at least partway from his taut mood; yes, the smile faded as quickly as it came, but traces of it still hung around the corners of his mouth. "I want a tree in my apartment. I thought we could get one here for old times' sake."

He pulled up to the squat wooden building that housed the office, probably once a storage shed on the original farm. They emerged into the cold and trudged through snow toward the entrance. J. L. Clarke's Tree Farm. The sign was still there, red lettering on a green rectangle, tilted to one side now, and in need of a fresh coat of paint.

Joe Clarke had been at UW Madison with Annabel's father. Every year Annabel and her brother and Dad— sometimes Mom, too—had come here early in December to cut a tree. After Dad died, Mom had bought an artificial one, even though John, in horror, had volunteered to come up from Florida and harvest a live one for her.

No, Mom thought it was time for a change. Annabel thought her sensible. Why hang on to traditions when those you shared them with were gone? Time to make new ones, adjust to life's shifts. No point living in the past.

She peered at her watch as they clomped up the wooden steps. Breakfast at the inn had been delicious, but it was nearly eleven and Quinn had promised to have her home by noon. So this would have to be—

Quinn grabbed her wrist on their way into the building. "I dare you not to look at your watch again until you get home."

Annabel rolled her eyes over a half smile. "You think I'm hopeless, don't you."

"Hopeless, no. Obsessively deranged, possibly."

She laughed and preceded him into the familiar, rough room, where her steps slowed. Dozens of bow saws hung on hooks on the back wall. Across from them the doughnut machine sat quiet today, but the usual hot cocoa steamed in a big black pot with a silver lid, the sweet scent of chocolate mingling with pine. At their entrance, a tall, broad-shouldered white-haired man stepped out of an inner office and grinned.

"Annabel Brightman, as I live and breathe." Joe Clarke extended a large, rough hand to shake, then pulled her in for a back-pounding hug. "How great to see you."

"It's great to see you, too, Mr. Clarke." An unexpected lump threatened to make an appearance in Annabel's throat until she swallowed it away.

"Joe, call me Joe." He beamed at her, his lined face still handsome, eyes still piercingly blue under bushier-than-ever brows. Annabel had always thought he looked a little like Paul Newman and adored him for it.

She introduced Quinn, then she and Joe chatted, recalling old times, old friends, people she hadn't given a thought to in years.

"I miss your dad." Joe took off his Green Bay Packers hat and clutched it in his weathered fingers. "I guess you do, too."

Annabel nodded, not wanting to speak. The light touch of Quinn's fingers on the small of her back told her he was, once again, tuned into what she was feeling. It was comforting and unnerving at the same time. Like a wonderful twin and a loss of privacy all wrapped up together.

"Well." Joe cleared his throat and put his cap back on. "Hardly anyone around today, with the snow and it being a weekday. I'll send a wagon to drop you wherever you like, or you can walk. There's a field right out back with trees ready to cut."

Annabel sent a glance to Quinn, who nodded, understanding her silent question. "We'll walk, thanks, Joe."

They picked out a bow saw with a chipped yellow handle and trudged on the snowy wagon track to the field just beyond the barn, where they turned in among the straight lines of Fraser firs. Annabel wandered down the row, remembering her father striding ahead, saw on his shoulder—he brought his own, naturally—eyeing the trees, challenging her and Joe to see if they could spot the best one. He always claimed the right tree would speak to him. And he always did pick the perfect one, the perfect shape and height, with just enough room between its topmost branch and the ceiling for the gold lit star their mother loved.

The trees will tell you, you've just got to listen. Same way you've got to listen to yourself, to your own heart.

As a teenager, she'd rolled her eyes behind his back. Trees talking to you, asking to be picked? Right. Sure, Dad. Millions of men in the world and *she* got the weird one who talked to trees.

Now, in his figurative footsteps, inhaling the piney perfume and the more elusive smell of snow and cold, she felt a nagging longing for something she couldn't precisely identify, and half-seriously let herself listen, walking through the silently falling snow, an occasional cold kiss that turned too quickly to wet on her cheek or nose. Instead of trees, however, she found herself mostly aware of the man beside her, who seemed as comfortable wandering around an orchard as he did tasting wine in an exclusive restaurant.

She smiled at him, grateful for the silly stocking hat and the unglamorous sweats he'd provided, keeping her toasty in the windless cold.

"Happy?" He grabbed her hand and swung it back and forth.

Absurdly, though she'd never admit it. "This is a nice surprise, Quinn. Thanks."

"You're welcome."

"You came here the year you were with us. Remember how my dad used to say the right tree would signal you to choose it?"

"I certainly do." He tugged on her hand, pulling her closer.

"What do you think. Hear anything?"

He looked around at the neat rows of Frasers. "Now that you mention it, I did hear 'Take me, now, please,' but I kind of hoped it was you."

Annabel laughed and took a couple of playful steps away so their arms stretched nearly horizontal. "Maybe it was."

"Oh?" He pulled her back again. "Tell me more."

She grinned at him, loving the cold, loving the warmth of her body in the chilly air, loving the spicy familiar scent of the firs. She didn't get outside enough. Most people didn't. They spent too much time avoiding nature, rushing from car to office to supermarket to home. Spending time like this, outdoors, then going home to a steaming mug of—

Oh, my gosh. She stopped in her tracks. What a *per-*

fect idea. She could bring clients here in early December, have them pick out a tree, then serve them cocoa or hot cider or buttered rum with cookies or tea sandwiches or—

"I see him too." Quinn spoke quietly. "He's stunning."

He who? She turned distractedly to see where Quinn was looking, rummaging for her cell to call Stefanie.

"Don't move." Quinn put a hand to her arm. "He'll fly away."

Fly, huh? She followed his gaze through the snow-flakes to a red cardinal perched on a branch ten yards down the long row, brilliant scarlet against the snow-covered green, like the one and only perfect Christmas ornament the tree needed.

The bird turned profile, eyeing them, head making jerky little movements as he apparently sized them up. Another male flew to a nearby branch; a less brightly colored female joined them. Annabel stood still, watching the birds watching them, and in a weird intuitive moment, felt this was her tree. The one Dad would want her to pick.

She rolled her eyes to shake herself out of the bizarre trance. Make that *Quinn's* tree. She wasn't getting one. And birds sitting on branches didn't mean the tree was signaling her to choose it; it meant the birds wanted to sit there. That was their bird thing to do.

"That's our tree."

Annabel jerked her eyes toward Quinn, already walking toward the fir. Had he felt it, too? Or was he joking?

"I guess it is." Her fingers became aware of the phone she still clutched in her pocket. She pulled it out and dialed her office number, turning her back on Quinn's inevitable disapproval.

Voice mail picked up—Stefanie must be on another line or occupied; Annabel had checked in before breakfast to make sure today's client was covered, so she knew Stefanie was there.

She started to leave a message, then glanced over her shoulder at Quinn, still with his back to her, looking the tree over, shaking snow from its branches, his broad shoulders and turned-up collar in stark black contrast to the green-and-white backdrop.

Annabel wrinkled her nose. Talking loudly on the cell would be grossly out of place in this quiet lovely spot. Despite what he might think of her, she could still appreciate that. The phone got punched off; she let it drop back into her pocket and joined Quinn at the tree. Her idea wouldn't go anywhere in the next couple of hours while she was his hostage. And it was way too late in the season to do anything but plan the events for next year anyway.

"Want first crack at it?" He held the saw out to her, eyes uncharacteristically warm, which did something a little funny to her insides. With her luck he'd seen her put the cell back and was all caramel-gooey and proud, thinking he'd reformed her.

Well, okay, he did have something to do with her disconnecting the call; she'd give him that.

"Sure." She took the saw and bent down to find the best cutting angle—not easy with the tree's low-growing branches.

Fifteen minutes later, with Quinn's efficient and her fairly clumsy efforts, they'd managed to cut the tree down and drag it triumphantly back to the office, where Joe refused payment over Quinn's insistence, and Quinn made arrangements on his cell for someone—she pictured a manservant named Jeeves—to come pick up the tree later that afternoon and deliver it. Oh, it must be so nice to have everyone jump when you said jump. When Annabel told people to jump, they returned the favor and suggested Lake Michigan.

But someday. She'd have a whole army of jumpers.

They got back into the Lexus, bringing fresh outdoor scents into the car's new-smelling leather interior, their toes and fingers gradually warming with the heating engine. Annabel pulled off the stocking cap, hunched her shoulders, then let them drop, leaving the dreamy atmosphere and memories behind, feeling as if she were returning to the present after visiting another time.

"That was fun, Quinn, thank you."

"You're welcome." He pulled his seat belt across his body. "I enjoyed it, too. Though I noticed you couldn't help having an intimate moment with your cell in the middle of it."

Of course he'd noticed. "Oh, yes. Well, the trip wasn't time wasted after all, I had a great idea for new business."

He stopped buckling. "Time wasted?"

Annabel's stomach dropped. Why had she said that? "I didn't mean it like that. I'm sorry. I really did have a great time."

"Okay." He clicked the buckle into place. "What was your idea?"

"Taking people in late November or early December to chop trees here, then take them back to their homes for hot drinks and finger food. They can decorate the tree right then, Christmas cheer, candlelight, fa-la-la…" She waited triumphantly for his reaction.

"Sounds perfect." He put the Lexus in Reverse and turned it around in the driveway. "Just out of curiosity, when did this brilliant idea strike you?"

Annabel frowned. "Why do you want to know that?"

"Humor me."

She shrugged. Okay. "Well, I don't know exactly. It popped into my head when we were looking for a tree."

"When you stopped walking?"

"Yes." She nodded enthusiastically. "That was it. You'd just seen the cardinal and I had no idea what you were talking about because the idea had just hit me."

He shifted into First and started off down the driveway. "I don't know why I'm surprised."

"What? What do you mean?" She couldn't tell where that came from. How come the intuition stuff only went one way? She'd love a close-up glimpse into his brain.

"I thought you'd stopped walking because you were overcome by the mysterious and eerie beauty of the tiny scarlet messenger your dad sent to tell you which tree to cut."

Annabel opened her mouth, then closed it because she had no idea what to say. Messenger? Was he serious? He believed in that stuff?

And he made her sound so…cold, and…unromantic. She wasn't *that* bad. Was she?

"Oh. Well. I guess I was preoccupied."

"I guess."

"If it's any consolation, I did think about the birds being a sign."

"And?"

"Dismissed it as silly superstition and made my call. What did you expect from evil workaholic Annabel?"

He shook his head. "You're a piece of work, you know that?"

"Who, me?" Annabel grinned and dug her cell out of her pocket, poked it on and started dialing. "Well, I knew enough not to start yakking business out there, but now I *do* have to call Stefanie and—"

A light tug, and the cell phone disappeared from her hand into his. "No calls. You belong to me until lunch, and I'm planning to eat late today."

"I *belong* to you?" She'd never in a billion years admit it, but the phrase had produced a tiny thrill in places that absolutely should not be thrilled by the concept. "As in your personal property? Your slave? Your—"

"Yes." He lifted an eyebrow and glanced at her, utterly deadpan. "Me Quinn. You Quinn's woman."

Annabel burst out laughing. He turned off the phone and returned it to her, obviously enjoying her amusement.

"Oh, my gosh." She let out a stray chuckle. "That nearly killed me."

He came to a stop at the intersection of highways JK and JJ. "You should flirt with death more often. Take a look at yourself."

"Huh? Why? I have hat head?"

He pointed to her window visor. "Do it."

"Yes, *sir.*" She pulled down the visor and peered into the mirror.

My goodness.

Eyes lit, cheeks pink—well, nose pink, too, but hey, it was freezing out there. She looked…joyous. Radiant.

"You need to do this more."

"Chop trees?"

"Yes. And whatever else I can get you out to do."

"Ha." She folded her arms across her chest. "I told you, this is it for daytime fun. No more. Nada. Finished. Zippo."

"We'll see." He turned onto E. Capitol Drive in the village and parked on the street. "Not that I object to fun at night, you understand."

"Mmm, me neither."

Quinn switched off the engine and sat, watching the snow accumulating on the windshield. Then he turned, eyes dark and serious, the way she'd come to think of him looking most often, with the sexy intensity that turned her brain to polenta. "But I want more than that."

Annabel sucked in a long, slow breath. "More?"

"More than just your nights."

She frowned. What, he wanted her at his beck and call all day long? "You can't have more than that."

He took his hand out of its glove, caught her chin and leaned forward. "Are you going to fight me every step of the way, Annabel?"

"Absolutely." It was all she could do to get the word out. His face was so close she could see the tiny lines in his lips, the speckles of black on his smooth-shaven jaw that would turn it near-gray by afternoon. She wanted him to kiss her so badly her lips were practically buzzing.

He released her chin, sat back in his seat and passed his hand through his thick dark hair. Then he turned toward her again, eyes amused.

"I look forward to it." He pulled the handle on his door and shoved it out. "Let's take a walk."

She took a long, calming breath to regroup, then joined him outside with a bright smile, knowing she should fuss about getting home, but not caring enough to start.

They put the charged moment behind them almost immediately, strolling down the quaint commercial street, careful on the snowy sidewalks, trading memories of times Annabel nagged John hard enough to be included on his after-school trips into town with Quinn—usually when her mother had insisted the boys let her tag along. She'd felt so special and grown-up riding in the car with them, even though they'd teased her most of the way—or John had mostly. They'd bought groceries for her mom or stuff for school, and always stopped at Penny's Candy Store for something sweet.

Her friend Tanya owned that store now. She'd refused to go in with Annabel's plans. Annabel was "too ambitious. Thinking too big." As if there were such a thing. But okay, fine. Tanya could sit here on the corner and sell bonbons to kids for the rest of her life if that's what she wanted.

They were approaching the shop now, a wide storefront—wider than she remembered. Had Tanya expanded?

Yes. Annabel gazed through the windows, spotless except for a colorful wintry painting of children building a snowman, and felt a strange sensation in her belly. Tanya had taken over the shop next door, which must have been the old typewriter repair shop—no big surprise that went out of business.

She'd kept the original half as a candy store, but this was not the old banged-up plastic bins of penny candy Annabel remembered. This was all glass and brass and rows of dark and light chocolate. The commercial sugary stuff was still there, but now it was laid out in tasteful brass buckets, with black scoops and clear Plexiglas lids. Dried floral arrangements dotted the counters, holly and herbal and cedar wreaths hung on the walls, and a white wicker reindeer pulled a miniature Santa's sleigh across the floor by the counter.

The other half of the store had been converted into a café, with delicate lacy black chairs and matching small round tables. The chalk menu listed—in perfect third-grade-teacher handwriting—cookies, scones and muffins, three flavors of freshly brewed coffee, hot chocolate and two fruit-blended drinks. Colorful boxes of tea lined the counters. Patrons sat sipping coffee, reading the paper or chatting.

The place spelled warmth and cheer and homey comfort. And even on a weekday morning, there were people in and out, some lingering to chat with Tanya, who was laughing at something a woman had said to her. She looked great, relaxed, happy, slender and chic, her blond hair in a new wispy do that flattered her pretty features.

"Let's go in."

Annabel opened her mouth to say she'd rather keep walking when the door was held open for her. Quinn stood waiting, and there was no way she could refuse without making a fuss. What would she say? She and Tanya hadn't parted badly. Well, not *that* badly. They'd just wanted different things.

She marched into the warm coffee, chocolate and cinnamon-scented interior and sent her sweetest candy smile to Tanya, who sent a sweet one right back.

"Annabel, how great to see yo-o-u!"

Annabel gritted her teeth behind her smile. She'd never been overly devoted to the way Tanya drew out certain words. "You, too, Tanya. The place looks incredible. You've done really well."

"Oh, thanks, I'm really happy with it." Her eyes went past Annabel and narrowed in flirty, exaggerated puzzlement. "Now you look just to-o-o familiar to be someone I don't know."

"Quinn Garrett. Long-ago exchange student at the Brightmans' my senior year."

"Quinn, of course!" She reached a beautifully manicured hand across the glass counter and shook—a little too long if anyone asked Annabel; but then nobody did. "It's great to see you, to-o-o."

The delicate tinkle of a bell and the sound of the front door opening ushered in new customers and a whoosh of cold air. Annabel could feel Quinn's eyes on her and she tried to relax. She was undoubtedly giving off tense vibes and naturally he'd pick up on it. He picked up on everything; jeez, it was exhausting. And okay, sort of thrilling.

"Hi, Mrs. Sacrost, and hi, little Timm-y-y-y."

"Hi, Tanya." Mrs. Sacrost beamed first at Tanya and then at the toddler in her arms. "Okay, Timmy. Now."

The little boy held out a wrinkled piece of paper with crayon scribbles on it.

"Oh! Is this for me-e-e?" Tanya took the paper reverently; Timmy snatched his hand back and buried his head in his mom's shoulder.

His mom laughed. "All week he's been asking to come and give you a Christmas picture."

"How sweet." Tanya pinned the scribbles to the bulletin board that hung on the wall behind the register, crowded with other kiddy pictures. "I'll put it right here, on our special kids board, oka-a-ay?"

Mrs. Sacrost smiled as if she were in the presence of her personal savior. "That would be wonderful."

"No problem. Oh, I've made up a bag of your family's favorites, to save you time this week. Does this look good to you?"

Mrs. Sacrost peered into the bag, made some ecstatic noises, paid and left with the now-beaming toddler clutching an on-the-house cherry lollipop.

The funny feeling in Annabel's stomach grew funnier…and less amusing. What was wrong with her? She was glad not to have this kind of shop. So dead-end. So…suffocating. Exactly the reason she'd backed out of their partnership.

"That was so sweet." Tanya smiled her stunningly perfect smile at Annabel. "So many kids were giving me cards at the holiday times I decided to start posting them."

"That's really nice." Annabel fidgeted and glanced around the store.

"Yes. I have a milk-and-cookies story time the first Monday of every month. The children come in with their moms in the afternoon. It's really fun. I get to know a lot of my customers that way, as friends."

"That's great." Annabel smiled and nodded, increasingly uncomfortable. That weird sadness, that empty strange feeling was at her again. She kept nodding. "Really great."

More customers came in and greeted Tanya, who gre-e-e-ted them back. Annabel really, really wanted to get out of here. She was uncomfortable, her mood was plummeting and she couldn't pinpoint why.

She felt Quinn close beside her. His arm slipped under her coat and stroked up and down her back, strong, warm strokes that immediately steadied her, made that strange panicky feeling dissipate. He might be freaky intuitive, but this time it helped immensely to know he was here and on her side.

"We have to get going." His deep voice cut through the female gabble; hallelujah, he had picked up on her need to leave, and she didn't have to say anything and risk betraying her discomfort to Tanya. "We just stopped by to say hello. I have to get Annabel back to work."

"Oh, how's that goi-i-ing?"

Annabel stretched her lips, hoping the smile looked more natural than it felt. "Really well. Holidays are crazy busy times."

"Tell me about it. All the shopping and parties and sledding with the kids, all the holiday events in the community…"

Annabel stared at her. Shopping? Parties? Community events? The woman had time to do all those things? Her business couldn't be going *that* well.

"Oh, wait, before you go." Tanya selected a long plastic-stemmed, red-foil-wrapped chocolate rose from a vase of them on the counter and handed it to Quinn, then winked at Annabel and gave a cutesy wiggly-fingered wave. "For the lady. No charge."

"Thanks, Tanya." Quinn ushered Annabel out into the blessedly fresh cold air. She took a few deep lungfuls, trying to clean out whatever weirdness had gotten into her.

"For you." He presented the chocolate rose with a slight bow. "Not to stop and smell this time, to stop and eat."

Annabel bowed in return. "Thank yo-o-ou, you're so swe-e-e-et."

Quinn quirked an eyebrow. "Looks like she's doing well for herself."

"Yes. This is what she wanted." Annabel rolled the chocolate rose back and forth across her lips as they walked back toward the car. "We almost went into business together."

"Let me guess. You wanted more than this."

"Yes." She braced herself. He was going to ask why and she'd have to justify her goals to him all over the place at a time she was feeling strangely vulnerable and didn't want to have to defend herself.

Instead he walked in silence until they reached the Lexus and he opened her door. "I'll take you home now."

Annabel blew out a stream of white breath, expecting relief at being able to get back to work, but the weirdness only got weirder. Home. To her beige office with the brilliant color of Quinn's flowers reminding her of this morning. Reminding her of him.

She put on a huge smile and slid into the car. "That would be great."

Except it didn't feel great. It felt…lonely.

6

QUINN PULLED BACK out onto the snowy road; the Lexus's back wheels spun briefly, then settled. He drove down E. Capitol slowly, adjusting for the occasional sliding, snow-induced detours the car wanted to make, then took a left on Josiah Street. Yes, he was taking Annabel home, but he had one more stop to make, one he wanted to make for her sake, but also in some way for his. Coming back to Hartland, revisiting haunts from the year he'd spent here, with the intention of reconnecting Annabel with her past, had brought memories back that had an unexpectedly powerful impact on him as well.

He'd thought of the Brightmans often over the years, called occasionally at first and sent a caed at Christmas for the better part of a decade. But he found it easier not to dwell on them, easier not to have to contrast that close, joyful experience of family with his own.

Now, the contrast had become something different and more profound. Rediscovering Annabel and trying to make her stop and take a look at her life had made him do the same. Yes, he had a good balance of work and enjoyment. Yes, he spent plenty of social time, played racquetball, tennis, golf, third base on the company softball team. Went to restaurants, dated occasionally, had a small circle of friends he could call to go see a movie or have a drink with when the urge struck, though he was and always would be a loner at heart.

But this connection with someone who knew him before he became an international commodity—this he didn't have in his seemingly perfect life. And hadn't missed it until he'd spent time with this aggravating, arousing, amazing woman he had known when he was barely a man, and hadn't had the luxury to appreciate since.

He wanted that luxury now, and damned if Annabel wasn't doing her best to keep him from it. *Would she fight him every step of the way?* He'd known the answer before the words left his mouth. What he hadn't expected was the question that popped into his head as he was asking.

Every step of the way…to where?

Annabel's self-actualization, was that all he meant?

No. He wanted more than just a physical relationship, all she seemed presently equipped to handle. Being around her, he felt like an underground-dweller finally given the chance for sunlight and fresh air. He wanted to break through to her surface, immerse himself in her, breathe her, feel her warmth on him in unlimited quantities.

Not have to manipulate and fight and plot to control, just to get her to spend the morning with him.

Did he respect what she was trying to accomplish with Chefs Tonight? Absolutely. He was the last person to insist or even think that she should settle for less than what she wanted. But the desperate need for speed, the impatience, the restless, angry yearning for what she was after spelled nothing but Napoleon-sized trouble to him. Goals were necessary, inevitable and important to anyone with a good business plan. But one had to enjoy the process, too, and he wanted to be in on her enjoyment. Go with her while she reached for what she wanted, and got it. As a friend, as a lover, as more—he still wasn't sure. But screwing her every night, between her last appointment or phone call or e-mail and her wake-up-and-start-in-again alarm, wasn't going to be enough for him. Now he had to make sure it wouldn't be enough for either of them.

Easier said than done.

He drove down Elm, past the corner where he and John and Annabel had waited for the bus to school every morning; past the empty lot where Annabel had caught John and him smoking and drinking beer and threatened to tattle unless they did her chores for a month; past the Larsons' yard, with the treetop clubhouse where he and John and the Larson kid—Larry—spent so much time and Annabel spent so much time pestering to be allowed in; and finally slowing to a stop outside her childhood home, where he switched off the engine.

The sight of the rambling two-story stone house brought on a swell of emotion. He glanced at Annabel, staring out the window, hand clutching her armrest, spine stiff.

He reached, touched her hair and was gratified when she leaned back into his hand. "When was the last time you were here?"

She lifted her head away. "After Dad died. John and I helped Mom move to her condo downtown."

"Would you like to get out and look?"

He saw the no forming on her lips, the same way he saw it forming when he'd asked if she wanted to go into

Tanya's shop, and immediately he opened his door and stepped out into the snowy chill, sure she'd be unable to stay in the car once he'd made the move. More manipulation, yes. No one had ever accused him of not trying to get what he wanted. But if he could help Annabel get past whatever she was afraid of, make her more aware of how she'd shut out most of her life, his theory was that she'd come willingly to him, and make the underhanded tactics unnecessary.

Until then, he needed some kind of control, not only over her, but over himself, to keep from rushing her.

Behind him, he heard her door open, saw her in his peripheral vision emerge from the car, come to stand next to him on the sidewalk, ankle deep in snow, and heard her take a long, deep breath.

He joined her, staring at the house, actually seeing it this time instead of scanning for her, staring at the bedroom window that had belonged to him, then at the one that had belonged to her. A vision came to him suddenly, transporting him back to seeing her face in that window when he and John had come home from some errand, seeing her smile and disappear and come downstairs, eager to find out where they'd been, what they'd done.

And suddenly and unexpectedly, other memories flooded him. Annabel crying in her room over some adolescent tragedy, how her tears had cut him, reminded him of his mom, made him want to protect her from everything that could hurt her. Annabel coming to his room in the dark while he was in bed, whispering about a plot she'd hatched to get John back for teasing her about some crush, begging him to help, giggling so hard she could barely get the words out. Annabel livid with her father when he took John and Quinn to his office for the day and left her home with her mom baking cookies. Annabel whooping it up outside with Archibald, the family's golden retriever, breathless and flushed; with Quinn indoors, all but pressing his nose to the windowpane, unused to witnessing or experiencing that kind of huge physical joy, wanting it for himself even knowing it wasn't possible for him.

"Good memories." She spoke softly next to him, low in her throat.

"Yes." He kept himself from turning to her, knowing he'd do something idiotic like take her in his arms and kiss her with everything he was feeling, in the process scaring the hell out of her and nullifying every chance he'd taken and every success he'd won so far. "What were you remembering?"

"Oh." She stiffened beside him, shifted her position and jammed her hands in her pockets. "Various things. What about you?"

Annoyance flared in him at her cowardice. He kept his eyes on the house, on her old bedroom window, and without thinking, he told her. All of them, leaving out only his wistful reaction to her giddy romp in the backyard. Maybe sharing them was a bad move, but right then he didn't care about the game, didn't care about control or whether it was smart.

He just wanted her to know.

When he was finished, he did look at her, unable to keep himself from her reaction, and found her wide-eyed, troubled, hand to her chest.

"They're all about me."

He gave a brief nod. "All about you."

Her eyes widened further; she licked her lips. Quinn turned back to the car. He recognized panic when he saw it. Yes, it had been a bad move, and congratulations. Now it was up to him to become as detached from the scene and from her as he'd just been immersed in it. He'd make no more progress with Annabel this morning. She needed to get home as fast as possible, back to her monochrome office and endless duties, so she could try to lose herself again in the familiar pressure of her daily routine. If he'd done his job right, she'd find it harder to concentrate, harder to disappear totally into her work. If not, he'd have another chance soon.

But one more push now would mean certain failure. And Annabel was rapidly becoming too important to risk losing.

ANNABEL RESTED her elbow on her desk, phone to her ear. Ring-ring-ring, was no one at work this afternoon? She was trying to follow up on a few queries for her Dinner and a Show events. So far things were going well for that program—though, as always, they could be going better. But honestly, a few snowflakes fell and people ran scurrying for home? She hung up in disgust. The stuff had still been falling when Quinn dropped her back here; piled up beside people's driveways, kids home for a snow day from school building a snowman across the street.

He'd dropped her off, with a peck on her cheek, a kiss that, in her still-agitated state, hadn't been a disappointment as much as a blessing. Too many memories, too many emotions, it had been a relief to get away from him and come inside to her own territory. Her own space, her own office, her headquarters. Never mind that the house seemed a little chilly today, and a scent memory of Tanya's chocolate and cinnamon compared unfavorably to something left in her kitchen trash too long. She was back. This morning had been an aberration and she was back in the groove. Or trying to be.

The phone rang; she squelched the idiotic girlish hope and picked it up.

Not Quinn. Her cousin Linda. Was everything on track for her husband's annual holiday business dinner at her house? Annabel rolled her eyes. Um, yes, Linda, exactly as prepared as the last time you called, ten minutes ago, or however long ago it was. Exactly as prepared as it was last year. Was Annabel still sure she couldn't join them on Christmas Day? Yes, Annabel was still sure.

She hung up the phone and it rang again almost immediately. This time she didn't allow the hope to manifest itself at all.

It was Mrs. Craven, cancelling her dinner party the following Sunday, Stu had the flu. Annabel expressed her sympathy for Stu and hung up, hating herself for immediately picturing an entire evening free to spend with Quinn. That was not the way to think. She could and *should* schedule in another Dinner and a Show that night.

She dialed another prospect number. Ring-ring, voice mail picked up and she left a brief message, giving available dates—she was nearly booked through New Year's. Next year she'd start earlier, give more options, hire more staff, maybe see if the symphony or the rep or the ballet might be willing to advertise for her. And she still needed to do something about attracting more traffic to her Web site.

A glance at the clock—four forty-five. Why did the afternoon seem to be crawling? Usually there weren't enough hours in the day, and she'd already lost a good many spending the morning with Quinn.

Not that she regretted it. Like eating a huge piece of chocolate mousse cake when you had pounds you could be losing—you might feel you shouldn't have, but you couldn't really regret it. Not totally. She'd had a good time with him, despite the hollow, strange moments at J. L. Clarke's without Dad, and at Tanya's homey, cheerful shop. And standing with Quinn in front of their old house.

She'd been totally unprepared for him to acknowledge so many memories. Even more unprepared for all of them to be of her. Not to mention the recitation had come out low, halting and intense, like a declaration he didn't want to be making. But a declaration of what? In seemingly typical fashion, he hadn't hung around to clarify. Had turned on his heel and gotten back into the car, driven her home in near-silence. Dropped her off as if he couldn't wait to get rid of her. Bewildering. As if he had an on-off switch or a circuit breaker that had tripped from some kind of overload.

More strange, listening to his memories had been like seeing herself as a different person, someone she wasn't anymore, someone she was surprised to find herself missing. That young exuberant girl who believed life was a set of open doors you could wander endlessly through.

Annabel roused herself. Come on. No one was the same person they were at thirteen. She shouldn't be mooning after the past; that was a sure way to remain dissatisfied forever.

She got up to get herself a glass of water from the kitchen and on the way back stopped by Stefanie's office, strangely reluctant to return to her own just yet.

"Hey. What's going on?"

"Oh!" Stefanie jumped and looked over from her work, dark circles under her eyes even more alarmingly dark than when Annabel had arrived earlier in the afternoon. "You scared me."

"Sorry." Had Stefanie lost weight? She looked unusually frail. "What are you doing?"

"Finishing confirmation letters for the new Dinner and a Show clients. Did you need me for something else?"

"Oh, no." Annabel waved her glass aimlessly. "Just coming over to see how you were doing."

Stefanie smiled pleasantly. "Almost done."

"No, I meant how you were doing…personally."

"Personally." She searched Annabel's face, as if looking for signs of psychosis. "Oh. Well. I'm fine."

"Good." Annabel took a sip of her water. "That's good."

"Yes."

Stefanie's heater went on. The chime on her computer indicated an incoming e-mail.

"Was there anything else?"

"Uh." Annabel shook her head. "No, not really."

"Okay." Stefanie sat looking at her warily.

Annabel forced a smile. Why was this so godawfully awkward? "Why don't you go home early today?"

"Oh." Stefanie glanced at the clock, which showed four fifty-five. "Thank you."

Annabel wrinkled her nose. "Okay, not that early."

"It's all right." Stefanie laughed. "Traffic will be a

zoo today with the snow. Five minutes will help. Thanks, Annabel."

"You're welcome." Annabel smiled tightly, feeling guilty for not thinking of letting Stefanie go home early before this. She lived in Waukesha, she had a half-hour commute even in good weather. "Drive safely. And get some sleep tonight."

"Why?" Stefanie paused in the act of shutting down her computer. "Is something big happening tomorrow?"

"No." Annabel gestured impatiently. Did Stefanie think she was that one-track? "You just look tired."

"Oh. Well, thanks." Stefanie bent and turned off her space heater. "I mean thanks for the wish to get good sleep."

"You're welcome." Annabel backed out into the hall and went into her office. Okay, that was weird. Was it that hard for Stefanie to believe Annabel just wanted to chat? Granted, she and Stefanie hadn't made great strides toward being close, and yes, that was probably mostly Annabel's fault, but she wasn't that much of a dragon-lady boss…was she?

Enough self-doubt. She was who she was; Stefanie seemed to like working here. They didn't have to be best friends to form an effective team. Annabel sat down at her desk and turned on her computer. The hologram burst over her desk and hummed while the computer booted up. When it was ready, she brought up a blank page on her word-processing program. She'd been wanting to brainstorm her Christmas-tree-cutting party idea since she'd been back today, but hadn't been able to settle down to it.

Okay. Now.

She typed "Christmas Tree Cutting Party" and saved the file.

So.

Her fingers drummed on the desk. Her gaze shifted to the flowers Quinn had brought, and immediately her thoughts drifted off in his direction. His rare smiles—was she wrong or were they becoming less rare? His warm, dark eyes. His equally warm and additionally amazing hands, pinning her against the B and B door. His talented tongue making sure she'd agree to spend the morning with him—and then some of the afternoon as well.

She brought her eyes back into focus on the flowers. Stop and smell the roses. Wasn't that what she'd done today? And where had it gotten her? To an afternoon where she hadn't accomplished squat.

Regroup.

She closed her eyes and took a deep breath. This was exactly why she didn't allow herself time off. The minute you slowed down, all you wanted was to slow down further. Sneak one chocolate from the box and you wanted to sit down, rip off the lid and devour the entire row. Then another, then another, then a long glorious wallow in box after box until you were utterly bogged down in the stuff. Paralyzed by your desire for indulgence.

One day with Quinn and she wanted more. She wanted two, she wanted a long weekend, she wanted three weeks in the Caribbean on a private island with nothing but food, condoms and a king bed for them to play on.

Damn.

Of course she knew deep down this was only temporary insanity. Her goals and her drive went much too deep to be supplanted in half a day. But the lesson was clear, and she'd learned it well.

No matter what kind of pressure Quinn applied— tongue, hands, or lips—this morning would be the last time she—

Her business line rang. She pounced on it like a starving woman on a free meal. Good. A business call. Something she'd need to deal with, something that would launch her back into the place she belonged, stop this silly mooning over—

"Annabel."

The deep voice went into her ear and traveled, electrifying and thrilling, all through her system. What had she *just* told herself about him? About her reaction to him?

"Hi, Quinn." She rolled her eyes. Gooey, breathless, teenybopper-crush voice.

"I can't talk long."

She lifted her chin. "Me, neither."

"Rosebud theater. Tonight."

"Well…" Chin higher. "I'll have to see if—"

"I'll be at your house at midnight."

Brows down. "Quinn. I'm not sure tonight is—"

"See you then."

The phone clicked off.

Annabel's mouth snapped shut from her next intended protest. She slammed down the phone and jumped to her feet.

She wasn't going to be one of his crew who jumped every time he said jump. Not only was it inconsiderate and rude, but she couldn't risk being seduced into spending more time away from work. Maybe tonight wouldn't be a problem—she didn't generally work past midnight—but what about tomorrow? Did he have plans to kidnap her again?

He was dangerous, devious; like a good strong marinade, he threatened to seep in and gradually take over her natural essence.

Tonight when he showed up, she'd just tell him… she'd tell him…

Her eyes lit on the stocking cap she'd tossed across the other chair in the room, on the Ho-ho-ho in green letters on the white brim. Her traitor brain again remembered too many details, too many thrills, too much of the warmth and excitement, a certain richness of existence when they were together, that she didn't have here in this barren room.

Worse, then a vision of the Rosebud theater, the red velvet couches where patrons sipped drinks and watched the movie.

Visions of what she and Quinn could do on those couches during the private screening he promised.

Oh, no.

Oh, no.

He'd said jump. And once again, she wanted to. But…

A slow, evil, thoroughly enjoyable smile spread across her face as the best idea in the world popped into her head.

She grabbed the phone. She'd need to call the owner of the Rosebud—she'd once done a party for him—then she'd need to go upstairs and rummage through a particular box in her storage closet.

This time she'd jump on her own terms. Yes, she did want to see him again, wanted to spend the evening in his magnetic and exciting and arousing presence. But her days of meekly playing his game were over.

Tonight was going to be her show.

7

ANNABEL PULLED ON a red-and-black flowery skirt that flowed to mid-calf, and a casual white scoop-neck cotton knit top. Underneath, she wore an ivory push-up lace bra. Thigh-high ivory stockings with matching lace garter belt. No panties.

She glanced at the clock. Eleven fifty-three. Just enough time to put on her makeup and jewelry.

After she'd made arrangements for the way the evening would go—i.e. her way—she'd finally managed to get some work done, though not much, then cleared the driveway of the finally stopped snow, come upstairs and taken a long, leisurely soak in the tub, buffing and shaving and otherwise making sure every part of her was presentable—and then some. She'd trimmed the curls between her legs to a short, sweet covering, painted her toenails dominatrix-red, and her fingernails to match. Taken extra time with her hair, so it fell in an attractive arrangement around her face and down her shoulders, glinting slightly auburn in the light.

Now she put on mascara, eyeliner, a touch of brown shadow at the corners of her eyes for a more exotic look. Quinn would be seeing her in dim lighting; she could get away with a heavier cosmetic touch than she usually used. Bright red lipstick next, thoroughly blotted, then blush, not that she needed much—her cheeks were flushed from the heat of the tub and from anticipation.

Jewelry next. She carefully extracted a pair of silver spiral earrings from the middle drawer of the miniature dresser Quinn had given her. The chest was perfect for earrings, rings and chain necklaces and she couldn't help smiling every time it caught her eye.

There. Eleven fifty-nine; she heard a car pull up outside and went downstairs, taking her time, enjoying the cool rush of air under her skirt.

Her doorbell rang. The atomic clock in Denver must have just ticked over to midnight; she couldn't imagine Quinn running on anything less precise.

Oh, she was going to spin his evening so out of control.

"Hello." She smiled coolly, not betraying the flip-flops her heart started doing at the sight of him. His black coat hung open; he wore a tux again and, oh, my, nothing black-and-white and edible had ever looked that appetizing. "Milwaukee must be pulling out all the formal-wear stops for you."

"Fund-raiser for the art museum." He took a step into the foyer. She didn't move back to give him room. "I was invited by the CEO of Herrn Brewing."

"How is the deal going?"

"It's going." He took another step forward so Annabel had to tip her head back to see his face.

"How much longer until it's a done one…?" She let the rest of her question go unsaid, *and you have to leave town?*

"Hard to say."

"Ballpark?"

"Can't even do that."

"Avoiding the question?"

He tipped his head forward slowly, until his mouth was inches from hers. "You look beautiful tonight."

"Avoiding the question." She arched a disapproving eyebrow over her pleased half smile and turned to open the closet behind her. "I'll get my coat."

Quinn drove them south on Sixty-third Street, right on North Avenue and the few blocks to the Rosebud Cinema and Drafthouse, where they parked in the lot adjacent to the building.

"I love this place." She walked next to him toward the entrance, bending her head into an icy gust of wind. "How did you hear about it?"

"I met the owner at a party, asked him if the place could be rented." He reached the front door ahead of her and opened it with a slight bow. "In a word—yes."

She preceded him into the dark foyer where to the right patrons could buy tickets, and to the left, beer, soda, popcorn and munchies and order pizza. She sent a surreptitious wink to the employee greeting them, a man named Jay she'd met earlier while making sure her own plans for the evening would happen.

They passed through the double doors into the dimly lit theater where rows of plush red velvet couches and love seats were interspersed with low tables. One couch in the center had been cleared around, and a table moved in front of it, draped with a white cloth. On the cloth, champagne flutes and a bottle chilling in an ice bucket; fresh caviar—undoubtedly beluga or osetra if Quinn was behind this—mounded in a crystal dish over cracked ice. A delicate china dish of salted almonds; a fine-textured pâté with dark shapes she guessed were truffles, sliced on a dark wooden tray and surrounded by melba toast and cornichons, tiny sour French pickles; a dozen oysters on the half-shell; finger sandwiches; tiny pastries; and a mystery dish with a domed cover. A single red rose in slender crystal vase added an elegant splash of color to the setup.

She smiled at Quinn. "This looks amazing. Thank you."

"You're welcome." He gestured her onto the couch and sat next to her—not close enough. She scootched over, feigning interest in the food, wanting Quinn to be very aware she was female tonight, very aware of the chemistry between them, since she planned to take full advantage later.

He pressed his thigh against hers, seeming to concentrate on taking the champagne bottle out of its bucket, but she had a feeling at least part of his brain was experiencing the touch. He opened the bottle expertly, the cork emitting a satisfying thunk rather than the huge pop that could mean spilling some of the precious liquid, and poured champagne for them both—be still her heart, Taittinger vintage.

Quinn lifted his glass in a toast. "Here's to good times. Past, present and future."

Annabel clinked her glass to his, sending him signals with her eyes that tonight would, indeed, be a very good time. "Here's to a really nice idea."

"It's a great movie. After all we accomplished today I thought we'd enjoy watching it and relaxing."

"Yes." She smiled into her champagne. Relaxing? Not entirely her plan.

"Did you get a lot done this afternoon?"

"Oh. Yes. I did." *Not.* But she'd never admit he'd managed to derail her so thoroughly. Nor could she tell him she'd spent some of that time planning tonight to blow his…mind. "I booked some Dinner and a Show clients. Caught up on some paperwork. Oh, and I lost one dinner party to the flu."

"What day did they cancel?"

"Sunday." She sipped champagne, pushing away the sneaking traitorous hope that he'd want to see her all evening.

"Let's see." He pulled a PalmPilot out of his jacket pocket and punched up his calendar. "Perfect. I want to book you for that night."

"Oh?" She tipped her head to one side, trying not to show her pleasure. "For what?"

"A small·dinner party."

"How small?" *Maybe two?*

"Four to six."

"Oh." Her pleasure dimmed slightly; immediately she chided herself. A dinner party was far better than a date. She'd get to put on a show for whatever important people he was entertaining, make some lucrative contacts for the future. "Happy to do it."

"Good. We can discuss menus another time."

"I'll e-mail you some options."

"Done." He put his planner away and handed her a small plate. "Now let's eat."

"It all looks incredible." She sent him a sly look. "But of course, being a woman who hates mysteries, I want to know what's in the covered dish."

"Ah." He held up a finger. "The pièce de résistance."

"What could possibly be any piècer than what's already out here?"

"Wait and see."

"I can't wait." She craned her neck forward as he took hold of the top of the silver dome and looked back expectantly.

"Are you ready?"

She nodded.

"You sure?"

Annabel laughed. "I'm sure, I'm sure."

"Voilà." He swept off the dome with a flourish worthy of a professional.

On the silver tray beneath sat a large candy bar, a plastic cup of fruit-on-the-bottom yogurt, and a box of unfrosted blueberry toaster pastries.

Annabel caught her breath and moved her hand to her chest. "What's this?"

"You don't remember?"

"I…yes. Of course." She laughed uncertainly. Every time her mom went shopping and asked if there was anything special the kids wanted, Annabel always said the same thing: Snickers, Pop-Tarts and Dannon fruit yogurt. And her organic-before-organic-was-cool mother always rolled her eyes. She made her own yogurt, Annabel could put jam in it, breakfast should be heavy in protein and fiber, and candy bars should be bought with her own allowance.

Quinn had not only remembered, so many years later, but made sure her silly childhood wish came true.

"Quinn…this is…it's probably the nicest thing anyone's ever done for me."

The minute the words left her mouth she felt like

cringing. For heaven's sakes. Plenty of people had done nice things for her. If she sat down and thought about it, examples would come positively rushing to her consciousness. In droves. She thought.

"What about the time your brother made up that beautiful song about you?"

Annabel burst out laughing. "Annabel the Cannibal?"

"That's the one."

She put her hands to her temples and shook her head. "How do you remember so many things about that year?"

"I paid attention." He shrugged, but the gesture didn't look convincingly nonchalant. "I paid a lot of attention."

"Why?"

"Because." His face started to go cold; his jaw tensed. "It was very different for me."

"Different how?"

"Just different."

"Okay." She took a sip of champagne to put off her frustration. So her life was an open book and his was bound and locked, key thrown off a cliff. "Will you always shut me out when I ask about your family?"

He held her gaze and, for a second, she thought she'd made him angry. Then he dropped his eyes to his glass and brought them back up noticeably softer. "Not always."

"When won't you?"

"You'll know."

She held up her glass, wanting to roll her eyes and growl at him. Why couldn't he answer any question straight out? She couldn't wait for *her* part of the evening to start, halfway through the movie. See how he liked having the control on her side. "Okay. Here's to then."

He nodded and clinked with her. "I'm sure many

more people would do nice things for you if you left yourself open to it."

It was Annabel's turn to shrug. A picture came into her head of the little boy handing Tanya a picture he'd made himself and she pushed it away. "Still trying to get me to change?"

He reached out and smoothed her hair, let his hand trail down her jaw. "Still trying to get you to change back."

Annabel frowned, remembering the feeling she'd had that morning, that the girl Quinn remembered was someone so different from who she was now.

She tossed off the rest of her champagne. People grew up, they evolved. Maybe he wanted her to be forever thirteen and gaga about the world, with all kinds of leisure to enjoy exploring it, but she wasn't. She was a grown woman running her own business. And she'd come here to do grown-woman things, not have her life examined again.

"Ready to watch the movie?"

Annabel nodded and Quinn took off his jacket, then his bow tie and cummerbund, undid the top two buttons on his shirt and rolled his sleeves up to the elbow and, oh, my God, the man was made for evening-clothes casual. He looked twice as sexy half-undone as he did dressed to the nines.

She took a long, deep breath, smiling at him. Yes, indeed, she was definitely ready.

He poured her more champagne, they loaded up their plates, then he signaled the projectionist. The room darkened, and *The Thomas Crown Affair* started rolling.

Annabel watched the intrigue unfold, swallowing oysters, savoring the truffle pâté and the caviar, crunching almonds, sipping champagne, the bubbly warm glow spreading through her, mixing with the glow of anticipation.

Yes, she was enjoying the movie, but all along she was hyperaware of the man beside her, of her nakedness under her skirt, of the soft red velvet underneath them. Pierce Brosnan and René Russo danced, parried, manipulated, two strong people unwilling to give an inch, both determined to stay on top of the situation and each other.

Gee, she couldn't think of any other couple like that.

Quinn put down his glass, placed his arm along the back of the couch and invited her in closer. She put her glass next to his on the table and moved toward him until they again sat thigh to thigh, a warm, strong connection.

"Here." He pushed her head gently so it rested on his shoulder while they watched, turned and kissed the top of her head, his hand idly stroking her arm.

For one aching second, she wondered if she'd made a mistake, if one-upping him in the manipulation department was really what she wanted out of the evening. This was so peaceful, so companionable. It felt so relaxed and so…right.

Then René Russo started her hot dance in the nearly see-through black dress as the frenzy of seduction took the film over.

The projectionist knew his job; it was too late to turn back.

Annabel had to be ready.

Pierce yanked René in for a kiss and the screen went dark. Quinn barely had time to tense beside Annabel, when right on cue another reel came up. It was one a passionate filmmaker ex-lover named Aaron had shot of her a few years ago, on a crazy night when they'd both been high on the arrival of the first springlike day and some very nice Meursault. Annabel had gotten the original back from him when they split, and though she hadn't watched the show since the night they made it, she remembered clearly how it had gone.

She stared at herself, up on the screen wearing a tight knee-length black skirt slit nearly to her hip on the left, and a low-cut clingy red top, laughing, a little nervous, waiting for Aaron to tell her to start. She remembered how shy she'd felt at first, how much wine and cajoling Aaron had employed to get her to do it.

"What's this?"

She felt Quinn's eyes on her and turned to smile sweetly. "Me."

He narrowed his eyes. "I can see that. But what—"

"Okay." Aaron's voice came from the speakers. "Let's do it. Go, Annabel."

Music started playing, a low drumbeat that filled the theater like a too-regular heartbeat. On the screen, Annabel started to sway, face turned to one side.

The drumbeat grew louder, then louder still, booming around the dark walls and couches around them, resonating in their chests. The on-screen Annabel raised her head, raised her arms and began to undulate her body.

Beside her, Quinn's breath went in, then he sat still and silent, no longer relaxed against her. Oh, he was going to enjoy this. She'd make sure of it.

Movie Annabel turned and presented her back to the screen, parted her legs in a bold, high-heeled stance and made frankly sexual circles with her hips, crossed her hands to her waist and lifted the top up and up...and over her head, revealing a naked back.

"Oh, God." Quinn's fierce whisper made something warm start glowing in Annabel's belly. This was good. This was going to be good. This was the right move tonight.

Chords chimed into the frenzied drumming, insistent, driving, guitars and synthesizer, some wild piece Aaron had composed.

On-screen Annabel responded, back still to the camera, flinging her hips and head side to side, long hair flying wild, gradually working the skirt down and off her naked bottom, kicking it to the side with strappy sandaled feet. She danced on, topless now, black garter belt and stockings, no panties, hair cascading down her back.

Beside her, Quinn's breath shot in and out in an irregular pattern. Perfect. Good. She slid her hand over to his thigh, brought it up to the hard bulge in his pants. Unzipped, unbuttoned, brought him out and slid off the couch, crouched down in front of him, put her mouth just over the head of his penis and circled him with her tongue.

On screen the music changed; the chords stopped; the drums slowed to loud percussive attacks. This was when she'd turned slowly to the camera, bare breasted, arms above her head, naked except for the garter belt and stockings, which hid nothing.

Quinn whispered her name and pushed his hips forward. She grasped the base of his erection with a firm hand and slid up and down, keeping the tip in her mouth, swirling her tongue over and over the head, tasting the beginning of fluid gathering already.

His body tensed and he made a guttural sound. His hands grasped her hair hard. She listened carefully to his breathing, to his sounds of pleasure, repeating whatever got the strongest reaction so she'd know how best to bring him close. The drums quickened again. She knew the camera was zooming in; her dance was getting wilder, she was touching herself, rolling her nipples, stroking her breasts, her hands traveling down over her own sex, where she would spread her legs for the final shot before the screen went suddenly dark.

There. One huge bang on the drum. There would be four more, then the close-up and finish.

Bang.

She took all of him in her mouth, down as far as her throat would let her, then back up, sucking hard, then down again, cupping his balls in her other hand, manipulating them gently. He groaned and let go of her hair, fisted his hands against the red velvet. This was perfect. Where was his control now? In *her* mouth, in *her* hands.

Bang.

Deep-throating, pulling back and working him with her hand, while her lips teased the top, then surging down again.

Bang.

Nearly time. She extracted a condom tucked in her waistband, unwrapped it while her mouth stayed busy.

Bang.

The end. Fade to black. She lifted the condom and prepared to roll it on him and climb on for the ride of his—

"What the hell is this?"

Annabel froze in a half crouch in front of him. He still stared at the screen, but he was not looking happy. Not happy at all. Strange sounds were coming through the speakers, moans and grunts and…her own protesting voice.

She turned around and gasped. The camera was still running, filming the wall where she used to be standing.

Apparently Aaron hadn't cut to black when he'd edited, as he planned.

Apparently Aaron hadn't edited at all.

So apparently she and Quinn were watching what the rest of the episode looked like after Aaron attacked her and pushed her back on the bed in his room.

Oh shit.

"Turn it off." She called out the words, even knowing the projectionist was gone, as he'd promised to be, and heard an eerie echo of her own words through the speaker. She turned back to the screen, confused until she realized on-screen Annabel had told Aaron the same thing at the same time.

Aaron came into view, reached toward them to switch off the camera, thank God, and the screen went dark.

And silent.

And so did the theater.

"Um." She dared a look at Quinn. "That last part wasn't supposed to be there."

"No?" He reached forward, grabbed her under the armpits and lifted her to lie back on the couch, lunged over her and covered her with his body. "No?"

"No. The shot was supposed to fade to black. The dancing is all I wanted to show you."

"I liked *that* part."

"I'm sorry."

He gripped her shoulders. "What are you trying to do to me?"

"Turn you on. That's all. I swear. It was supposed to be a surprise."

"It was definitely that."

"I mean a nice one."

He watched her for a moment, his breathing ragged, face strained. "Who is that guy?"

"I haven't spoken to him in years. I made him give me the film when we broke up. I haven't looked at it since he made it."

He closed his eyes and lowered his head beside hers. "Annabel…"

"I promise." She whispered the words, then hesitantly circled his back with her arms, praying he wouldn't pull away, wouldn't fight her offer of comfort.

He didn't. She held him, equal amounts of tenderness and self-loathing engulfing her. Nice job, Annabel. You won. Didn't let him have the upper hand. Rah-freaking-rah.

Except he played the same game, manipulating her, keeping himself closed off—she'd had sexual contact with him three times, but never seen him naked or been naked in front of him, never even kissed him for heaven's sake. Nothing that would make either of them vulnerable.

What a bunch of crap it seemed right now.

"Annabel." His whisper was a deep buzz next to her ear.

"Mmm?" She gave in to temptation and pulled up his shirt, stroked his smooth strong back.

"I hated hearing you with that guy."

She winced, squeezed tightly before she resumed stroking. "I'm so sorry."

"Did you love him?"

She felt herself tensing. He just wanted to know. It didn't mean anything. "No."

"Have you been in love with any of them?"

"No. Have you?" Her hands wanted to still on his back and she had to remind herself to keep their motion going.

"Been in love with any of your men?"

She smiled. "Any of your women."

"No." He lifted up onto his elbows to look at her, face closed, no longer showing the pain, jealousy, frustration, back to his old self. Quinn the smooth. In complete control.

She wanted him the other way. A man who felt things, a man who…cared about her. And showed it.

Oh, no.

She stared back, wondering what he was thinking, hoping he couldn't read the thoughts she was having right now. Because in spite of herself, she was fighting an irrational and arrogant desire to be the first woman he fell in love with.

"Do you think you ever will fall in love with someone?" Her voice came out a thick whisper, betraying her fear, damn it.

"I don't know. You?"

"I don't know."

He lowered himself back down, kissed her cheek, her temple, her nose—she knew better than to offer her mouth by now—then positioned his erect-again penis on her clitoris, moving it lazily back and forth. Then forward and back. Then in killer circles that threatened to make her crazy.

She moaned. What was it about him that turned her on so instantly?

"I used to be sure I never would." He replaced his penis with his fingers, dipping inside her, rubbing them wet all around her sex. Oh, he was an artist, the way he moved, varied his strokes. She went from turned-on to wild in a matter of seconds.

"What?" She moaned again. What had he said? Her body's clamoring for climax was interfering with her hearing.

"I used to be sure I'd never fall in love." He stopped touching her and lifted off the couch. She heard the tearing of a foil packet—thank goodness he'd brought his own—then he moved back over her, and pushed inside—only halfway, then out and half-in again, positioning his body in a way that made her nearly lift off the couch from the excitement.

"Oh." She clutched his shoulders, then did lift off the couch, straining her hips up to meet his teasing half thrusts, sweat breaking out on her body, the insistence growing stronger. "What…changed your…mind?"

He held back just as her climax neared. She moaned in protest, pushed her hips, on the edge, so on the edge…

"Quinn."

He thrust home, long, hard thrusts to the hilt. Annabel exploded over, crying out, pushing against him. His hips moved harder, faster, then she felt him coming, heard the deep breath and heard him whisper something she couldn't quite catch, though she thought she heard her name.

She lay under him, her breath still coming in hard pants, partly from the thrill, the exertion, and partly because it was hard to catch her breath with him on top of her. She didn't care. She'd happily suffocate if it meant she could feel his warmth on her, and his weight.

Instead, he pulled out of her, sat up, got off the couch to take care of the condom, and she braced herself, knowing what was coming next and already hating it.

"I'll take you home."

Damn, damn, damn, damn.

She got up numbly from the sofa and put on her shoes, adjusted her mussed skirt. Right. Home. Sex over, party over, done, finished. Just the way she liked it.

Until she met Quinn.

They found Jay, who declined their offer to help put the place back to rights and graciously accepted their thanks for helping out. Quinn drove them back to her house in silence and walked Annabel to her front door, waited while she opened it and stepped into the foyer.

"Would you like to come in?"

He shook his head. "I have a long day tomorrow."

"Okay." She tried vainly to hide her disappointment. What was she thinking? She had to get sleep, too. It was after two, and if she didn't make up for the lost day of work today, she'd…she'd…

Oh, no. She'd what?

She took a quick breath. Fine. Send him on his way. "Well. Thank you for the really nice day."

"You're welcome." He kissed her on the cheek and turned to go.

Weird panic hit her. "Oh. I'll e-mail you those menus."

Quinn turned back to smile, then again started on his way out the door. "Thanks."

"I have some new ones I can send, as well as the standard. And some holiday menus."

He turned again with a nod, then back to the door. "Those sound perfect."

"Thanks again for today. I had a really great time." She bit her lip. *Shut up, Annabel, you're sounding desperate.*

He nodded. Another step toward the door. "I enjoyed it, too."

Annabel took a step after him. "Did you know after you left, we never stopped calling your room Quinn's room?"

He turned slowly this time, looking at her intently, as if she was about to tell him something he'd wanted to hear for a hundred years. "Really?"

She nodded, looking at him stupidly. He'd done so much for her today. Brought her back to her childhood home, shared his memories, set up a fabulous evening for the two of them—even bought her Snickers and Pop-Tarts—and she'd been ungracious and rude, and then paid him back by trying to one-up him at the theater.

A sudden huge rush of emotion flooded her. One deep breath. Held. Then the memories she'd kept from him earlier today, in front of her childhood home, came pouring out.

"I remember you winking across the table at me when Dad criticized me for one thing or another and I was furious and sulky. I remember you cheering for me when I finally beat him at chess. I remember you finding me in my room, crying out some teenage misery or other. You sat down on the bed with me and you patted my back and you listened to me as long as I needed you to."

All those and other memories she hadn't thought of in years came tumbling out, until her voice ran thick and her throat dried up and she stopped abruptly, feeling vulnerable and trembly. Then tears came she didn't try to stop, but let them roll quietly down her cheeks, staring at his handsome face, wavering and indistinct for a moment, then sharpening back into focus when she blinked.

What the *hell* was the matter with her? PMS? Not enough sleep? Worry about work? What was happening to her? She wasn't usually emotional at all; in fact, she prided herself on her even temperament. Not the hormonally driven now-I-feel-it, now-I-don't type, not her. She must be missing her family, her childhood or something.

God, he must think her a total fool. She opened her mouth to apologize, when she noticed he was looking up toward her ceiling, smiling slightly.

She followed his gaze and caught her breath, jerked her eyes back to his secretive smiling ones. Mistletoe. How the hell did he get that—

A slight rustle, and the sprig dropped to the ground between them.

She stared at it lying on the brown tile, then looked up to see Quinn taking the one step toward her he needed to take before he—

Oh, my gosh.

His mouth was warm, perfect. He kissed her over and over, drawing her closer, wrapping his arms around her so she felt cocooned, enveloped, her head resting in the crook of his elbow, his mouth tasting her lips, over and over.

Oh. My. Goodness.

He came up for air and she looked at him, dazed, breathless. "I'm old enough now?"

"Yes." He grinned at her, kissed her again and grinned at her some more.

"I can't believe—the mistletoe—how did you get it up there?"

"Tiny elves."

"But then it fell, just like when we were—"

He put a gentle finger to her lips. "Better not to question magic too closely."

She laughed and he put his hands to her face, backed her up to the wall and kissed her. Kissed her again. As if now that he'd broken the kissing barrier, he wasn't likely ever to stop.

Which was totally, utterly and blissfully fine by her.

"Good night, Annabel."

"You can't stay?" She clasped his forearms and tugged him nearer.

"Another time." He kissed her forehead, then her mouth, and stepped back.

"Quinn." Her voice faltered, but she had one more risk she wanted to take tonight, since the rewards this far had been so damn good.

He turned around, still smiling; he seemed lit, energized in a way she hadn't seen before—and she had a feeling she looked the same.

"I asked you a question, back at the theater that you never answered."

A hint of the guarded look reappeared on his face. "What was that."

"I asked what happened to change you from being sure you couldn't fall in love to thinking you could."

"I did answer."

She frowned, thinking back. "No, I'm sure you didn't."

He gave a mysterious smile and stepped outside. "Think about it, Annabel."

She watched his black-coated figure stride to the car

parked in her driveway. She closed the front door, turned, and put a hand to the inner door into her living room, then stopped, thinking back on the evening. How had he answered her question?

They'd been making love. She'd asked him what had happened to change him—then he'd starting driving her out of her mind and he hadn't said anything until he whispered her name when he—

She gasped, closed her eyes and let a thrill of fear and joy burn through her. Her name.

The answer to what had happened to make him think he could fall in love was Annabel.

8

ANNABEL TURNED into her driveway, the minivan full of groceries for Cousin Linda's husband's holiday party the next night. Evan worked in insurance like Annabel's father. Every year he invited his choice business associates over to a holiday dinner. Last year he'd loyally invited Chefs Tonight to provide the food. Obviously she'd done well enough to be invited back.

She was going to have to haul ass this afternoon; she'd overslept this morning, then had to run to the Henneckes with one of the emergency stews she kept in her freezer when unexpected company had shown up and they needed dinner. And, of course, once she got to their house, they'd wanted advice and to plan other menus and so on and so on. Then Sentry hadn't had oysters for tomorrow's soup course, and she'd had to make the trek to Sendik's out on Capitol—suffice to say she was behind. Very.

And not the least because Quinn kept ringing her cell when she needed to be getting things done, wanting to find out what she was up to or talk dirty to her, or generally be the most enjoyable pain in the ass she'd ever encountered.

She stopped the van outside her back door, shifted

into Park and pressed the button releasing the liftgate. She had to unload the groceries and get a leg up on cooking for tomorrow's party before she went to the Metro Milwaukee Association of Commerce After Hours event tonight at Maggiano's. She'd be up late again finishing preparations, and another huge day tomorrow.

Men and business didn't mix. Especially unbelievably sexy men who were heaven in the sack and fun to talk to as well. She'd pay one way or the other eventually. It was a good thing he wouldn't be in town too much longer.

Even though it didn't feel at all like a good thing.

She unlocked her back door, propped the storm open wide, grabbed a fistful of plastic grocery bag handles and dragged as much as she could carry in one trip out of her van. Stefanie was at Linda's helping set up the house; usually she'd come out to help.

"Hey, lady."

She turned to see a small boy running up her driveway, so bundled up against the cold that all she could see were a few patches of freckled skin around his eyes under his navy face mask.

"Come see our snowman!"

Annabel smiled painfully. Yeah, that's exactly what she wanted to do right now. "Sorry, I'm really busy."

"It's totally cool."

"I'm sure." She took the bags inside, deposited them on her kitchen floor and went out again.

The kid was still standing there. "It has a button nose."

"No kidding." She picked up another load, took it inside and made the trip out again.

"And two eyes made out of coal."

"Wow. That's great." Another load, the last one if she really carried a lot. When she walked back outside to pull the van into the garage, he was still there.

She put her hands on her hips. Would it be too rude to say Go away?

Yes.

"Guess what else it has?"

Annabel rolled her eyes but found herself wanting to laugh. "Corncob pipe?"

"Straw braids and a Viking helmet." He smiled cheerfully. "Her name is Brunnhilde."

She shut the liftgate on her van. "That must be some snow…person."

"Yeah, come see."

She started walking toward the driver's side door. "I can't."

"Why?"

"I told you, I'm busy."

He scowled—or at least she thought he did, from the little she could see of his face. "Stefanie came and saw it."

Annabel stopped in the act of reaching for the door handle. "You know Stefanie?"

"Sure." He started turning back and forth, like the agitator in a washing machine, letting his arms twirl with his momentum. "She has lunch with my mom."

"Who's your mom?"

"Kathy." He said the name as if there was a big *duh* waiting to happen right afterward, but he knew enough not to be that rude. "She has a day care in our house. You didn't know that?"

Annabel took a deep breath. Okay. Thirty seconds.

She could look at the snowman and then go inside. It wouldn't kill her. "Let's go."

"Awesome."

They crossed the street to where the snow-Valkyrie stood, obviously made with help from Mom. Truly, she was an impressive specimen. Annabel admired her properly and felt almost warm and fuzzy when the boy beamed with pride.

See? That was painless. And she could tell Quinn what an absolute angel of kindness she'd become. "What's your name?"

"Jackson."

"Well, Jackson, thanks for showing me Brunnhilde."

"Sure. Maybe you could have lunch with my mom and I could show you my Yu-Gi-Oh! cards like I do Stefanie. Blue Eyes White Dragon is her favorite, but I like Feral Imp."

"Okay." Annabel backed off, nodding. The angel of kindness was pretty much over it now. "I'll remember that."

Kathy came to the door to call her son in and Annabel waved and hightailed it back to her side of the street before she got caught in a conversation with Mom and had to hear more about the Christmas Eve block party. Cute kid. How weird that Stefanie was having lunch with Annabel's neighbors and Annabel barely knew their names. Nor did she have any idea Kathy ran a home day care across the street, though that would explain the noise.

Back inside, she unloaded the groceries and put them away, washed her hands and leafed through her stack of recipes. She could make the soup today except for the cream and oysters, and heat it through at Linda's tomorrow.

She banged a pot on her front burner and tossed half a stick of butter in to melt, then went over to her counter to chop the fennel bulbs she'd left there. After the soup, she could put together some of the stuffing ingredients for the Cornish hens, then bake the chocolate sponge cake for the Bûche de Noël. That, she could assemble tomorrow.

Her cell rang. Annabel smiled; the smile became a chuckle and then laughter. She carried the cutting board over to the stove and dumped the chopped fennel to sizzle in the pot before she dragged the phone out of her pants pocket. What did she say was one reason she was so behind?

Because *someone* wouldn't stop calling her. Because *someone* seemed to have taken their movie date last night as carte blanche to contact her whenever the mood struck. Which seemed to be every twenty seconds.

"Hel-lo-o-o." She made her voice extra singsong so he'd know she was on to him, and went to get her headset so she could talk hands-free.

"What are you doing?" His low, deep voice sent the same warm shivers over her that it did every time.

"The same thing I've been attempting to do all day, trying to get something accomplished."

"What's stopping you?"

"Some freak keeps calling me."

He inhaled sharply in false alarm. "That is bad news."

"Mmm." She stirred the fennel, smiling like an utter goofball, then measured a quarter cup of fennel seeds into her mortar.

"What are you going to do about him?"

"I don't know." She pounded the seeds with her pestle, smile drooping. That was more truth than she wanted it to be. A brief article in the *Milwaukee Journal Sentinel* business section—which she hadn't read yesterday or today, and shame on her—had noted that talks between Holocorp and Herrn Brewery were nearing successful completion. Which was a lot more than Quinn had told her, and which meant Quinn would have no further reason to be in Milwaukee, at least in the short term. Maybe he'd come visit again when the new factory went on line, or when he was needed to boost morale, but soon he'd be going back to live in California, in his no-doubt gazillion-dollar mansion near San Francisco, while his minions took over here.

And that would mostly likely be that.

"I'm actually calling for a reason beyond the fact that I am constantly overcome with lust thinking about you."

"Oh?" Her smile found fresh life. She added the fennel seeds to the pot, lowered the heat and gave the vegetables another stir, inhaling the licorice aroma dreamily.

Concentrate on your work, Annabel. She risked flying off into gooland when he talked like that.

"A friend of yours is coming to town."

"Santa Claus?"

"Guess again."

She scowled. A friend of hers? Who did Quinn know that she was friends with? Someone from junior high? Oh, she hoped not. More ghosts from the past she did not need right now. "I give up. Who?"

"Adolph Fox."

"Adolph Fox?" She stepped back from the stove, wooden spoon raised like a flag. *"Adolph Fox?"*

He chuckled. "No, Adolph Fox."

"Oh, that's fabulous!" She covered the pot and brought the mortar and pestle to her sink, dunked them in the bowl of soapy water at the ready for her *mise en place*. "What is he going to do here?"

"A promotional tour."

She frowned. See what happened when she didn't keep up with the paper? "Appearing where?"

"He's promoting a new line of low-carb frozen pizzas and is appearing at Holidayfest activities downtown in conjunction with a certain enormous local brewery launching a new low-carb winter ale."

"Diet beer and pizza, how Christmassy."

"Since when do you concern yourself with how Christmassy something is?"

She rolled her eyes. "Ho, ho, ho."

"So…"

"Ye-e-es?"

"On to more important things."

"Such as?"

"What time I can see you tonight."

"Oh, Quinn." She sighed and pulled a potato out of the plastic bag on the counter for peeling. "I can't tonight. I've got soup to make for Linda's party, then I have an After Hours event at five at Maggiano's, then back home to make stuffing and cake and I should get a start on the hors d'oeuvres and I really need to get a decent night's sleep for once."

"Okay. I'll be over at seven-fifteen."

"Quinn."

"To help." His voice became warmer. She closed her eyes to enjoy it and nearly peeled her thumb. "I'm a decent cook, I can give you a hand with the menial stuff—be your slave in the kitchen."

She put the peeled potato down and crossed to stir the vegetables on the stove again. It had never occurred to her he could help. Her relationships with men in recent years had been strictly confined to bars, restaurants and bedrooms. If he came over, she'd be letting him into her life in a much more intimate way than by letting him into her—

Ahem. On the other hand, he could do things like wash lettuce and chop parsley, make the watercress dip, help out with a ton of the prep work. It would make a huge difference to her level of stress and the amount of sleep she'd be able to get tonight.

And she'd have company. And that company would be Quinn.

He started whistling the theme from *Jeopardy* and she smiled. He knew exactly the battle that was going on in her, damn him.

"Stop that."

"Just providing my own hold music."

She laughed. "Okay, okay, you can come."

"Mmm, I plan to."

"Come *over*. Quinn, this is going to be business, not pleasure."

He sighed. "Annabel, if I manage to introduce one concept in your skull by the time I leave…"

She rolled her eyes, ignoring the kick in her stomach at the word "leave." "That would be…?"

"That you can actually have both at the same time. Business and pleasure. And in this case…"

Silence. She craned her head forward expectantly. "Mmm?"

"I want you to have both as often as possible. With me."

ANNABEL WALKED into the high-ceilinged bar at Maggiano's Restaurant and made her way to the upstairs room where the MMAC event was being held. Five o'clock, the party was just starting, and already quite a few suited men and women were ordering drinks and launching themselves down the road toward tipsy networking. Annabel made her way to the bar and requested seltzer with lime; she held her alcohol well, but this evening she was too tired and pressured for booze. And in a business setting, when she was trying to make an impression, she didn't want that impression to consist of slurred babble and too-loud laughter.

She cast an eye around the attractive room—gas fireplace on one side providing warmth and atmosphere, hot and cold hors d'oeuvres on another, providing sustenance and a speed bump to alcohol absorption for those driving home. She sipped her seltzer and made careful note of the better-dressed women in attendance. Sad to say, even now that wives were putting in equal time at the office, the decisions about cooking for the family each week generally still rested solely on their shoulders.

So she wanted to approach females first, preferably those wearing wedding rings. A family of mom, dad and kids meant the value of the contract went up. The more the merrier. After that, she could branch out to men without rings, since busy bachelors often wanted a home-cooked meal as well.

A likely looking brunette stood alone near the fireplace, mid-thirties, hot-pink suit, rock the size of Gibraltar. She looked confident, in control, someone Annabel would like to know.

She walked up to her and smiled, stuck out her hand. "Annabel Brightman."

The woman blinked. "No kidding, really?"

Annabel blinked back. "Uh, do I know you?"

"No, but—"

"I do."

Annabel turned at the sound of the familiar voice. Oh no. Ex-lover Bob. Whose calls she'd dodged for so long.

"Hey, what a surprise." She shook his hand, trying very hard to make herself sound pleasantly happy to see him, and wasn't sure she succeeded. The last thing she wanted to do was have to fend him off all evening.

"Why, it's Annabel-who-doesn't-return-calls." He rolled his blue eyes and grinned.

Annabel gestured stupidly. "Oh, well I was—"

"Busy, I know." He slid his arm around the attractive pink-suited brunette. "This is Karen Adleman."

"Karen, nice to meet you." Holy cheezits, Bob had a new woman—a *fiancée* if the ring was anything to go by. *That* was a quick courtship. But hallelujah! Annabel was off the hook.

Except why was he still calling her?

"Karen is starting her own Web-design company and is offering design work at a reduced rate, to get the buzz going around town." Bob looked at Karen adoringly, then back at Annabel. "So I remembered you complaining that you wanted to upgrade your site, and I thought you'd be a perfect candidate."

The lightbulb flashed on in Annabel's brain, and what it illuminated wasn't pretty. "Is that why you've been calling?"

"Yes." He shook his head as if she was beyond all hope. "I couldn't get past the big freeze-off to tell you."

Annabel felt herself flushing and attempted an apologetic smile at Karen. "I…that is…"

"It's okay. The main thing is that we've hooked up here, so if you're agreeable, I can show you some of my work so far." Karen extracted a card from her purse and passed it over. "Here are the Internet addresses."

"Okay. Good. Great. Bob's right, I've been wanting to redo my site, lure in more traffic." Annabel pulled herself together, cheeks still burning. Oh, nice. Bob had been trying to help both her and his beloved here, and Annabel assumed for no particular reason that he wanted back in her pants. Worse, she'd been a total bitch.

Well. Hadn't she come off sweet as a lemon in *that* encounter.

She forced herself to keep chatting to show no hard feelings and smooth things over, but she couldn't help keeping only one eye on Bob and Karen, the other working the room again. Which prey to pounce on next?

A few likely women were sprinkled around the room. When she felt she could exit gracefully, she excused herself and spent the next hour pitching her services— starting with the requisite small talk, then getting around to the point of the evening as far as she was concerned. Damn shame she couldn't just march up to someone and state her business, see if there was a need and if not, move on. Waste of her time to bother chatting someone up only to find she or he had no interest.

By six-thirty, she was without success and beginning to get antsy, anxious about what still needed to be done tonight, and wanting to go home. But the point of these two hours was to drum up new business, so drum she would.

She grimly marched up to yet another executive-looking woman and started in again. Hi, I'm Annabel, what do you do? Oh that's nice, I have a personal chef business, did you know that when you factor in the time you save shopping and cooking and cleaning up, my services don't end up being that expensive, bla-bla-bla-bla-bla.

The woman's elegant features froze under her upswept blond do. Annabel sighed. Okay. Fine. Don't need me. Don't want me. Whatever. She felt like taking the woman's shoulders and shaking her and yelling, "I do really good work and I can make your life easier, what is your problem?"

The buzz in the room grew suddenly louder, and people seemed to be milling more excitedly. The elegant woman looked around, clearly longing to escape Annabel's evil neediness, then her frozen features melted into a stunning smile over Annabel's right shoulder.

"Hello."

The deep voice flowed over her, and oh, she knew who that was. And more to the point, why Ms. Ice Maiden in front of her had suddenly morphed into Lulu the Love Goddess.

"Hi, Quinn." She kept her voice cool and professional while her insides struck up a yee-haw hoedown. "This is—"

She gestured desperately at the blonde, completely unable to remember her name. Of course she'd only met about ten thousand people tonight…help!

"Jeanette Wakefield." The voice dripped honey all over Quinn while her glance at Annabel contained artificial sweetener.

"Oh, yes." He shook her hand warmly. "We met at the Art Museum fund-raiser. How's Boris doing?"

Jeannette positively sparkled. "Much better. The vet said it most likely wasn't diabetes, possibly just an allergy."

"Good news. And by the way…" He reached into his inner jacket pocket. "I found that article on the Cook Islands I told you about and printed it out. I've been carrying it around on the off chance I'd bump into you again."

"Oh, *thank* you." She took it from him, beaming. "This will be a huge help. Bruce and I are still weighing our vacation options, but I'm so glad to know about this place."

"You're welcome. Tell Bruce I also included an article about online cigar stores for him."

Jeanette seemed to find this hilarious. Annabel stood and smiled politely, feeling utterly superfluous.

"Excuse me, Mr. Garrett?" Dark-suited man, about fifty, short, in ill-fitting suit. No wedding ring. Possible candidate.

"Call me Quinn, please, Tom. How are you? How did things go last week with Johnson Controls?"

"Very well." He beamed, clearly thrilled to be included in the group of Those Quinn Smiled Upon. "They asked me to do up a proposal."

"Excellent." Quinn put his arm to the small of Annabel's stiff back and brought her forward. "I'd like to introduce you to a friend. Tom Denato, this is Annabel Brightman."

"Nice to meet you." Tom Denato shook her hand. "What's your line of work?"

Aha! "I have a personal chef business, Chefs Tonight."

"I see." He took a sip of his drink, throwing a glance at Quinn as if he'd much rather be talking to him. "And what does a personal chef do?"

"All your weekday cooking and grocery shopping. I show up at your house one day a week, prepare the following week's meals according to menus you choose and portion them in packages for your freezer. I even clean up after myself."

"Well. I had no idea such a service existed." He glanced at Quinn again.

"It's very convenient. Are you interested? I have a card I can give you. I also do dinner parties and have some special holiday events you can host. I do all the work— you just provide the booze, show up and enjoy the party."

He began looking a little tense and took a step back. "I don't think I need anything like that."

She sighed behind her polite smile. "Okay."

Enough rejection. She wanted to go home. With Quinn. Cook up a storm and get back on top of what she needed to accomplish.

Another man broke into the circle and said hello to Quinn, who remembered where they met, every member of the guy's family, where he'd been on vacation the previous year…

Someone else entered the circle and brought Quinn a drink.

Another person brought him a plate of hors d'oeuvres.

He listened, commented, laughed. Everyone seemed to fascinate him, everyone's career, family situation, hobby. No one seemed to notice he shared nothing of himself.

Must be nice to be so on top of the world that you could spend time chatting and didn't have to go chasing after people. She was pretty sure that, over the next half hour, one by one the entire room came up to see him. Everyone loved him and he seemed to love them all right back.

At seven o'clock, an enormous scattering of beeping watches announced the event's end and a general exodus began. A few lingered. Quinn had a few plants in someone's garden he hadn't discussed yet, so he was talking—or rather listening—to a dull-eyed, middle-aged woman as if she were the most fascinating creature he'd ever encountered.

Annabel had no idea how he did it. She would have run screaming from the room ages ago. By now, though, he was probably used to it. It must come with the territory.

"Such a nice man." A female voice spoke behind her. "You feel like there's no one else in the entire world when he's talking to you. No wonder he did so well for himself."

"Exactly, Doris." Another female voice answered. "You don't get the feeling it's all about the money for him."

Annabel rolled her eyes as they passed. Of course it wasn't about the money for him. He had practically all the money in the world. That was hardly the point anymore. He could sit back, relax and enjoy it. Though why he'd consider coming here part of that enjoyment, she hadn't a clue.

She downed the last of her seltzer, wishing she had something much stronger. But the time ahead of her tonight that she needed to spend around knives and open flame made drinking alcohol unwise, to put it mildly. She didn't need her concentration messed with.

As if being with Quinn wouldn't do an even more effective job.

He came toward her, through the last lingering members staying for one more drink or planning to eat at the restaurant.

"Ready to go?"

She nodded, feeling tired and spent and a little cranky. Actually she'd been ready to go about ten minutes after she got there. And striking out with everyone she'd spoken to hadn't helped her outlook.

"Nice people." He escorted her out of the meeting room, putting his arm to her back to let her precede him through some tables in the restaurant.

"Yes."

They went back downstairs through the bar and Quinn followed her out the revolving door into the chilly parking lot outside Mayfair Mall. "What's wrong?"

"Noth—" She caught herself and took a breath of the wintry air. "I wasn't in the mood for that today."

"Any particular reason?"

"It just seemed like…well, maybe people weren't in the mood for me."

"I am, if that helps."

She laughed. "Thanks. It does."

"Where's your car?"

She pointed and Quinn walked with her down the

long row of cars crusty with road grime and salt, many with snow still clinging to their roofs.

"The way you talked to Tom…" He glanced at her and she tried desperately to remember which one Tom was.

"Tom?"

"Fiftyish, graying hair, single, works for a multimedia company, had a presentation last week to—"

"Yes, okay, I remember." She stopped him before he could go on to recite shoe size and underwear preference. "What way I talked to him?"

"Is that how you present your business to people?"

Annabel bristled. Doubtless he was trying to be helpful, but she wasn't in the mood for that kind of helpful right now. "What about it."

He wrapped his arm around her shoulders, stopped walking, pulled her in close and bent his head so that she could have kissed him with almost no effort if she were so inclined. And once she caught the barest hint of his scent, she began to be. Shamelessly inclined.

"If you show more interest in the person you're talking to than in yourself, they will show more interest in you." He leaned in as if to kiss her, then drew his tongue in a squiggly line across her lips and made her—she couldn't believe it given her advanced case of the grouchies—giggle. "That's today's lesson."

"Thank you, teacher." The words came out hard and ungrateful and she closed her eyes. "I didn't mean to sound bitchy. I'm sorry. You're probably right."

"I'm always right."

Her eyes shot open and found his teasing ones, which melted her indignation immediately. He moved his hands under the opening of her coat, brought her body flush against his and kissed her, his mouth soft and warm against her wind-chilled lips. "So does this mean we get to play teacher tonight?"

She pretended to give that a deep mull-over. "Would I have to be the naughty schoolgirl?"

"Hmm. That has possibilities." He smiled, but his eyes stayed dark and serious. "People want you to be fascinated by them. Everyone needs that, and it's not hard to act that way. Then, mercenary as it sounds, you can get what you want out of them more easily."

"Catching flies with honey?"

"Exactly."

"So, are you just acting fascinated with me right now? So I'll play your kinky sex games later?" She tipped her head coyly back, anticipating his answering zing.

Instead, his eyes grew darker and more serious. "I'm utterly and genuinely fascinated by you, Annabel."

Oh, my God. She took in a long breath. "Me, too."

"Fascinated by you?"

She laughed. "You."

"Good." He brushed back a lock of her hair the wind had decided to fling into her face. "Mutual fascination is good."

He kissed her again, long and slow and sweet, and something went a little crazy in Annabel's heart.

It didn't take a professional chef to figure out that whatever simmered between them was on the verge of being heated into a full, rolling boil. And she couldn't decide if she wanted to pull back to maintain the temperature, or turn the flame up higher and risk getting overcooked.

9

QUINN STARED grimly at the cherry desk in his nearly dark apartment. Somehow afternoon had passed into evening almost instantaneously—and damn early—and he had yet to turn on any lights.

After the initial high of being with Annabel yesterday, first at the After Hours event, then blissfully chopping and stirring and mixing—who knew cooking could be that fun and sexy and stimulating?—his mood had plummeted. He'd felt anxious and uneasy through this morning's meetings, and an afternoon catching up with his assistant in California. He'd only called Annabel twice today, respecting her need to stay focused on her cousin's party, but even that hadn't done much to make him feel lighter.

But then everything about his feelings for Annabel were new and confusing, so welcome to the damn club. The night they'd watched *The Thomas Crown Affair*— or attempted to watch it—had given him his first taste of jealousy. Nasty bitter stuff, he was glad to have avoided it before this. In the past, on the rare occasions a woman had tried to make him jealous, he'd either been amused or turned off.

Until the sound of Annabel doing who knew what

with that Aaron character had filled the theater, and a rage he could barely control had filled him. Not rage at Annabel, at least not once he registered the horror on her face and believed she never intended him to experience that part of the tape. But rage at the man who had touched her, at the pleasure he gave her, at all the things they'd shared that would always belong only to them.

An utterly irrational waste of energy, as utterly and irrationally beyond his control as his own heartbeat. It had taken all his efforts to beat the fury down, convince himself he was being ridiculous and get the evening back on track. But the damage had been done, his own vulnerability exposed to him on a marquee lit with blinding lights. When they made love finally on the red velvet couch, he wasn't thinking of his own pleasure, wasn't thinking of how she made him crazy with lust or how badly he wanted to come inside her.

He'd been thinking of how much he wanted their time together to be calmer, effortless and intimate. How much his need to see her had less to do with her and more and more to do with how he felt about her.

After the sex, he hadn't wanted to escape the way he always did, to keep emotions and the relationship sharply defined and easily contained. He'd wanted to lie there, lust sated, and experience her. Smell her, touch her, talk to her and watch her answer.

Of course then, with sick irony, the fear she might not want that too had brought on the same need to escape he'd finally avoided, and he'd bolted from the couch. Until he knew whether her emotions were growing along the same lines as his, he wasn't going to leave himself open for that kind of smack-down.

Look at him, Mr. Extreme Caution. Until Annabel allowed herself to verbalize memories of Quinn in her young life, he hadn't even felt safe kissing her.

He turned on his desk lamp; the light made a warm yellow circle on the white blotter and pushed the rest of the apartment farther away into darkness. He picked up a piece of paper from the desk, the printout of an e-mail from his assistant. He made a diagonal crease and folded the extra along the bottom, then tore it off so the paper became a perfect square. He couldn't remember the last woman he had kissed like that. Maybe there had never been a woman he had kissed like that. Maybe only the very first came close, Cornelia Lieder, a friend of John's from Hartland High School—and she'd barely begun to emerge from girlhood.

A few more folds and the shape of a bird began to emerge from the paper, origami he'd picked up from a business trip to Japan where he'd had the privilege of living with a local family instead of in a hotel.

He could stay in Milwaukee a few more days. But he wasn't really necessary to the negotiation process even now, hadn't been for some time. He could have shown up a week ago, gone to a few parties, stayed a few days making nice with the natives and flown home to California. One person had changed his plans and Quinn wasn't known for being tremendously flexible with his schedule.

Worse, that one person had put thoughts of more plan changes in his head. Thoughts that involved a move to Milwaukee, of making the facility here dedicated to research and development instead of manufacturing. A division he could head up, reimmerse himself in the creative side of the business and leave the day-to-day CEO running of the company to someone else.

Crazy. After one week. Except the dissatisfaction had been building for a while, dissatisfaction he'd carefully suppressed. It had taken Annabel—his feelings for Annabel—to bring it to his attention.

The bird's head emerged, long beak, graceful neck, thick body, a swan, or a crane. A discreet chime came from his laptop, indicating some task had come due on his calendar program. He put the bird aside and drew the laptop closer.

Call Mom. He stared thoughtfully at the message. Not until this moment had it occurred to him that the regularly scheduled electronic reminder to call his mother was an indication of how rigid his own life had become.

Only one thing felt rigid around Annabel, and she had a way of taking care of that rather quickly.

He picked up his phone and dialed home. His father had long since left. He'd rotted away his liver in some other woman's house and died a few years ago, mostly unlamented by his only child.

"Hi, Mom."

"Right on schedule. I can set my watch by you."

He frowned. Up until today, he'd taken her first line of their every-week chat as a compliment. "How are you doing, Mom?"

"Fine. The new hip works much better, thanks to you and all your money."

He couldn't help smiling. She never missed the opportunity to take shots at his billions, and never seemed to mind when they made her life easier or better or simply more enjoyable. "I'm glad the surgery helped. Did the new laptop get there?"

"Yes. And the tray, so I can work at it in bed. That was thoughtful, son. Now I can surf the Net with the best of 'em."

He grinned, imagining her in their tiny house, which she refused to move out of, surrounded by more luxury items than she had ever known existed, let alone dreamed someday she'd own. She'd kept the living room the way it had always been, apart from new upholstery and carpets, so as not to appear to be—in her words—inviting the Lord's wrath with way more stuff than a decent Christian woman should have.

None of which sinful stuff she refused.

He was delighted. Considering what his dad had put her through, he wanted her remaining years to be as pampered and luxurious as possible. "How's Hank? Still proposing?"

"Every month, regular as church. Damned old fool."

He chuckled at the affection in her voice and got up to turn on the lamp next to the couch. "So love burns brightly still."

"He's good to me. More than your father could imagine even on his best days."

Quinn pictured his mom and Hank sitting together in the family room on the new sofa, watching one of the reality shows his mom adored on the wide-screen TV he had bought her, holding hands, quiet and content.

"Mom, I—" He broke off, appalled at what he'd been about to say.

"What is it?" Her voice sharpened into parental alarm.

"Nothing's wrong." He held up his hand as if she

could see the placating gesture. "I was just going to tell you something."

"And?"

"And I changed my mind."

"You have some disease."

"I'm healthy as a horse."

"Then you met someone."

He took a deep breath, crossed back and sat again at his desk. Since when did he think he could hide anything from her? "Yes."

"Took you long enough. I was starting to think you were gay."

"Not gay. Selective." Or something. He nestled the phone between his ear and shoulder and picked up the origami bird to give it long, strong wings. "Remember Annabel Brightman?"

"Ah, still."

"What do you mean, still?"

"You came home from that year talking of nothing else."

"I did not."

"Humph. Fine. You know best, I'm sure."

He finished the bird and set it on the desk, where it balanced perfectly, wings spread slightly as if it were itching to take off and circle the room. "It's not…I'm very…she won't—"

His mother's laughter cut him off. "I like this girl already."

"Thanks." Quinn rolled his eyes good-naturedly.

"Let me guess. She won't drop and give you twenty when you order her to like every other person you encounter in your life?"

"Something like that."

"Well, that's a blessing. I was afraid you were going to start thinking you could walk on water the way people treat you."

"No worry, you keep me humble."

"So what's the problem?"

He tightened his lips. "She lives here. I live in California."

His mother scoffed. "What's the real problem?"

Quinn frowned. Picked up another piece of paper—a thank-you from the American Cancer Society for his last donation—and began folding an airplane, a model he'd designed as a boy.

"Hey." His mother's voice became gentle and sweet, the way she'd talk to reassure him after one of Dad's violent outbursts. "Sad to say there's not a damn thing you can do about the way she feels except be your own sweet self. And even then, no guarantee she won't bust your heart in a million pieces. But I tell you, you can sit in that office and make billion-dollar decisions by yourself for the rest of your life, or you can get out there and do something important. Tell this girl you love her and give her a ring and a houseful of babies and make yourself happy. God gives us precious few opportunities for happiness. When one comes along, you grab on and ride for all it's worth or you're a damn fool."

She muttered a few extra sentiments under her breath, which weren't exactly flattering to him or his gender. Quinn grinned to gain power over the lump in his throat. Good old Mom. She'd waited a long time to grab her own happiness, had kicked his father out of the house only after Quinn went off to college—and he'd only agreed to go if she promised to get rid of Dad. No way would Quinn have left her alone with him.

"Okay."

"Okay what?"

"Okay, tomorrow I'll tell her I love her and give her a ring and a houseful of babies and—"

"Right, Mr. Smart-ass. Just don't be scared to live, Quinn. That's all I'm saying."

"Thanks, Mom."

"You're welcome. Now get the hell off the phone, my soaps are starting."

"I'm gone. Take care."

"*I* always do. It's *you* I worry about."

"You're my mom, worry is what you do."

She chuckled. "I'll see you soon, Quinn, you coming tomorrow or Christmas Eve?"

"Christmas Eve. In the morning." He grimaced, guilty he was cheating his mom for one more night with Annabel.

"See you then. I'm glad you met someone. I hope she deserves you."

He hung up the phone, and laughed bitterly. He'd done the impossible, revolutionized technology and the world, brought to the reality of people's everyday lives what many said would remain only in science fiction, and he was utterly stumped how to start bringing emotional intimacy to a relationship.

But to admit failure now would be to make the kids at school and his father right about him. That he would always be odd, cold and alone. He'd already lived too much of his life fulfilling their prophecy. Able to make small talk with anyone who came along, but crippled when it came to real sharing. Ironic, of course that the person who had accused him, his father, was the person who had the biggest hand in cutting that part of him off. When home wasn't safe, it was hard to grow up warm and trusting and open.

Which is why that year in Hartland had been like falling into a Candy Land version of life, and why he'd clung so tenaciously to those memories. He'd been a different person with the Brightmans. And he wanted to become a different person with Annabel.

He pulled his laptop closer, opened the hologram screen and his e-mail program. He needed a break from thinking about her. Sooner or later, he'd figure out what next step to take. Often solutions came to him when he stopped clouding his brain with thoughts and let it do its job unfettered by consciousness.

He scanned the list of incoming mail, spam and business and—like a sign that stopping thinking about Annabel was going to be impossible from now on—an e-mail from her brother, John.

To: Quinn Garrett
From: John Brightman
Date: December 22
Subject: Christmas
I know this is last-minute, but Alison and I wondered if you'd like to fly down to Orlando and join us for Christmas. I called Annabel and it sounds like she's planning to be her old Scrooge-y self and sit home alone. I wasn't sure if you had other plans.

I guess you guys have been seeing each other here and there. Am I crazy or did I detect that there's something more than just palling around going on? I promise I won't show up with a shotgun, quite the opposite, I would be thrilled.

Let me know about Christmas.

Best,

John

Quinn read the e-mail a second time, then a third. Then hit reply and started typing.

To: John Brightman
From: Quinn Garrett
Date: December 22
Subject: re: Christmas

Hello, John. Thanks for the invitation. It's very generous of you to open your family's home to me at Christmas. However, I'll be visiting my mom in Maine as usual. I'll make it a point to travel to Florida in the New Year so we can get together.

I have been seeing a lot of Annabel. She's a unique individual and I hope I have been doing her some good. She's had the same effect on me.

Thanks again for your invitation. My best to your wife and children.

Quinn.

Quinn reread the note. *I hope I have been doing her some good. She's had the same effect on me.* He closed his eyes. As usual he *wasn't* saying more than he *was.* Which in business was often a very smart strategy. Let your opponent talk, give him silences nerves would force him to fill. Make him risk divulging things he shouldn't. Keep your own hand close, no tipping, the old poker face.

But this wasn't about business. What had he told Annabel about mixing pleasure into her business? He needed to separate business from his pleasure.

He picked up the paper airplane, launched it, watched it glide gracefully across the room and slide to a smooth landing on the Oriental rug, exactly in the center of an ornamental circle. With all due respect to his mother, it was a little early for I love you, marry me, have my children. But for the first time in his life, he could see that as a possible outcome of a relationship.

Which meant he couldn't keep acting as if Annabel's transformation was the point of them getting together. He had some transforming to do himself. He needed to open up to her, make it clear that happy-ever-after was something he could see evolving out of what they'd barely started, see how she reacted and whether she could see it, too. Stop shutting her out from so much of his life and his past. Tell her who he was and what he wanted, from his life and from her.

He scrolled back up into the body of the e-mail. Positioned his cursor after "She's had the same effect on me" and typed, "In other words, I'm falling for her like a boulder shoved off a cliff."

He grinned, chuckled, laughed out loud.

And hit Send.

ANNABEL CAREFULLY LADLED steaming oyster fennel soup into a two-handled cream soup bowl of Linda's Christmas china set. Cornish game hens sizzled away in the oven along with prosciutto, pine-nut stuffing. A medley of root vegetables flavored with ginger waited on the stove for a final reheating. Two fruit conserves already graced the sideboard in the dining room; a mesclun salad with grape tomatoes and Belgian endive waited for last-minute dressing before being served after the meal, in the European style. The Bûche de Noël was decorated, a rolled cake frosted with chocolate and made to look like a log, complete with meringue mushrooms dusted with a touch of cocoa powder. For color, she'd decorated the plate with sugared cranberries and mint leaves.

Everything was in place, on time, oh, she loved the satisfaction of running the show, putting on a really elegant, sophisticated good time. Everyone here would leave remembering the lovely party—and Chefs Tonight. With luck, orders would come in for her services from the guests and their acquaintances. Word of mouth was her very good friend. Now she just needed to spread it across the country.

Stefanie appeared from the kitchen for the next round of soup, her pleasant expression dropping off into exhaustion the second she reached the safety of the kitchen. Annabel handed her two more bowls, lips pressed together in concern. She wished she could spare Stefanie, who really looked like she needed to rest for about a month. But there was no way Annabel could cook and serve this meal by herself in a timely fashion at this critical stage.

"Stefanie, after the main course is served, you go home. You look exhausted. I can handle salad, dessert and cleanup by myself."

Stefanie turned her back to the swinging door into the dining room and started to object.

"No." Annabel lifted her hand. "No argument."

"Oh, but—"

Annabel shook her head quickly. "No buts."

"Okay." Stefanie's face softened into relief. "Thanks. That would be nice, I am kind of tired."

She pushed back through the door and into the dining room.

Kind of tired? No, not just kind of tired. Something more that that. While Annabel respected Stefanie's privacy, she was getting anxious about it. As Stefanie's employer, she had a right to know why her employee looked ready to drop on her feet. When the next quiet moment came, Annabel was going to ask her what was wrong.

She finished dishing out the last two bowls of soup, sprinkled the last sprinkle of chopped fennel fronds for color and put the cover back on the pot to stay warm, checking the burner temperature carefully to make sure the soup wouldn't boil. Then she hurried out to the doorway into the living room and caught Linda's eye, gave her the thumbs-up that they were ready for the guests to be seated.

Linda beamed her approval, then waited until the laughter died down from a joke someone had just told, and invited her husband's business associates to the table. Annabel stepped back from the doorway but lingered, watching the group file toward the dining room. The living room looked lovely, the tree especially. Linda had decorated it with tiny red papier-mâché apples, gold bells, glass icicles and white porcelain angels with elaborate corn-husk robes. Christmas music wafting from the CD player filled the room with warmth even now that the bodies had gone.

For a strange moment, Annabel felt that same homesick longing she'd experienced standing in front of her childhood house in Hartland with Quinn. Homesick for what, she hadn't a clue. Maybe she missed her parents, although she wasn't thinking of them in particular.

She had turned to go back into the kitchen when the sound of her name stopped her. Linda's joy-filled voice came clearly around the corner, talking to her husband, Evan.

"Yes, she throws a beautiful party."

"Just never goes to any." Ice clattered against crystal; Evan must have come back to retrieve and guzzle the last of his Scotch. "I don't know why you keep bothering to invite her for Christmas."

"Because she's family. Because I adored her parents and because I can't help doing whatever I can to try and break her out of that ice she's got around herself."

"Ha! Submit her to the Winterfest competition as a sculpture and be done with it."

Linda gave that comment a lot more hilarity than Annabel thought it deserved. "Oh, Evan, stop."

"Well, this apple fell so far from her tree she probably can't remember which one she grew on. Her mother was such a beautiful person. Gracious, kind, thoughtful…"

"Yes. Well." Linda sighed. "We can't all be our mothers. Let's go in. Soup's on and it smells delicious."

Annabel hunched her shoulders. Oh, wow. She hadn't had that much fun since high school when she found out George Borden's apparently flirty nickname for her, AK, actually meant "Amateur Kisser."

So.

Evan didn't like her and Linda thought she was heartless. How nice.

She stalked abruptly into the kitchen, her accomplish-things energy badly sapped.

"What's wrong, Annabel?"

Annabel smiled reassuringly at Stefanie, feeling even lower. Oh, that was nice. The second Stefanie sensed a change in Annabel's mood, she asked, while Annabel had gone weeks now noticing Stefanie radiated all the health and happiness of a death-row inmate, and Annabel had barely mentioned it.

"I'm fine. But I really want to know what's up with you, Stefanie. You're losing weight, you're pale, what is it?"

"Oh, I—" Stefanie gestured randomly, obviously at a loss what to say.

"Okay. Look, I don't want to pry. I'm concerned about you, that's all."

"Thanks." Stefanie bit her lip, looking as if tears were about to burst forth.

"You're not…sick are you?"

"No." The tears spilled over. Annabel hurried for a tissue and thrust it at her. Okay, subject closed. She couldn't afford to have Stefanie sniffling through the next course. The guests would think—

Annabel stopped herself. Patted Stefanie awkwardly while she blew her nose. God, listen to herself. Worrying about what the guests would think when her friend was falling apart. "You're not having trouble with Frank, are you?"

"No, no, nothing like that."

"Okay. I'll stop asking. But if you want to talk… I'm here."

Stefanie barely masked her surprise, then sniffed gratefully and blew her nose again. "Thanks. I'm fine. Really. I promise."

"Good." Annabel grinned at her as cheerfully as she could, not at all convinced. "In that case, lay out the dinner plates and let's start loading them up. Dinner's coming."

The soup bowls came back in, the hens went out. Stefanie left after Annabel practically shoved her out the door to her car. The hens came back in, salad went out, salad came back in, the Bûche de Noël went out—to appreciative gasps Annabel was thrilled to hear—then espresso and brandy in the living room, after-dinner chocolate, crystallized ginger, dried apricots and dates, pecans and ribbon candy. Any excuse to keep the waistlines expanding, blood alcohol levels rising. And for those driving, caffeine to combat the sleepiness of the overload and the hour.

Then finally time to go home for the guests, and cleanup time for Annabel.

Linda and Evan went upstairs to bed with effusive thanks that Annabel received as graciously as she hoped her mother-that-she-wasn't-at-all-like would have received them.

Back in the kitchen, the last dishwasher load done and the last crumpled cocktail napkin and pistachio shell rounded up and thrown away, Annabel wiped down the counter, wrung out the sponge and glanced at the bird clock on the back wall. Nearly one. Too late to see Quinn, though she hadn't planned to anyway. But her nights had become defined by whether she'd be with him or not. And she found herself less and less willing to think past the night in question, to all the "nots" ahead of them when he left.

A few trips to the van to load it with the things she'd brought over earlier, then she stood in the hallway, zipping her coat, putting on her gloves…and staring at the tree, still lit in the darkness of the house. She ought to turn it off.

Ten steps into the middle of the room, she stopped and stared more, unable to pull the plug just yet. The tiny clear lights made the needles of the tree glow green in bright circles, and the glass ornaments sparkled rainbow colors. The angels had their perfect pink mouths open in song, hands wide as if to embrace humanity, corn-husk robes dyed in subtle earthy colors.

A lump formed so hard in Annabel's throat, she felt she was trying to swallow past a cement ball. She backed away into the hall and let herself out into the soft chill of the night. The serious cold snap was over—all day she'd heard the constant drip of snow melting in the direct sun, seen the icicles forming off of Linda's roof through the kitchen window.

Now, on the way back to Wauwatosa, she kept noticing Christmas—houses rimmed with icicle lights, crèches and Santas glowing in people's front yards. The town seemed peaceful this late, holiday shoppers home in bed, kids probably already having trouble sleeping, with the big day coming so soon.

All night and even now, she'd felt like a spectator, a disembodied ghost, watching the rest of the city celebrate a holiday that had touched only her pocketbook since her mother had died.

She pulled into her driveway, her house plain and

dark, into her garage, turned off the motor and rested her head on the steering wheel. A sudden fierce yearning for Quinn hit her with such force she nearly burst into tears.

Then the implication of what she wanted from him hit her just as hard. Not sex, not fun. She wanted him because she felt sad and lonely, and she knew he'd understand and fill the emptiness in her. Where other people saw in her an ice sculpture, he saw warmth and beauty and kept trying to get at it in spite of her every effort to keep him away.

She fumbled in her pocket for her cell, dialed his number, then shook her head and hung up before it rang, leaned back against the seat and blinked hard to keep tears from coming. It was nearly one-thirty. She had no business calling him this late just to whine. By tomorrow she'd be fine again, and this strange feeling would seem like a distant dream that had happened to someone else.

Car door open, foot on the ground, one step then another all the way into her house, double-locking behind her, clogs off on the mat by the door, up the steps, checking for messages, then a glance into the living room to—

"Oh!" Annabel gasped and put her hand to her mouth. Her living room. Transformed. A tree—the perfect size and shape—decorated with tinsel and bright ornaments; colored lights and strings of glass beads; a star glowing golden yellow on top. A red fabric Advent calendar hung on the wall next to it, with stuffed presents to take daily from numbered pockets and hang on the flat Velcro tree. A large stuffed Santa sat on her couch, grinning, sack on his back, which held tiny wrapped boxes. White frosted bells dangled from under the shade of her floor lamp.

She leaned in the doorway, trying to take it all in. Quinn had done this. She knew it with utter certainty. What she couldn't fathom was how he'd known this was so much what she needed today.

He was the most amazing man she'd ever met.

Her cell phone rang. She fumbled for it in a daze. "Hello?"

"Do you like it?"

"Quinn. You…it's so beautiful." She put her hand to her head, not even bothering to ask how he knew she was home, then stared again at the tree. "Is this the one we cut at Clarke's?"

"Yes." He chuckled and she managed a smile, loving that he laughed so much more easily now, and hoping she had something to do with that. "Were you surprised?"

"Completely." And overcome and dangerously warm and fuzzy at the thought of him doing this for her.

"You like surprises?"

"I like the ones you give me."

"Good. There's one more."

"Oh?"

"In your room."

She laughed. "Another tree?"

"Go up now."

"Okay." She took off her coat, tossed it onto the desk in her office and mounted the stairs. "What is it?"

"You'll see."

"Bigger than a bread box?"

"Much."

"Can I eat it?"

"Oh, yes."

"The world's biggest chocolate bar?" She reached the top landing and turned toward her room. Her lips formed an *O* of surprise.

Candles everywhere, the room glowed with warm light; Christmas music played softly. A tiny tree on her dresser, decorated with white lights and red origami birds.

"So?" His deep voice echoed in one ear on the phone…and, in the other, it resonated around her room. "What do you think?"

Quinn. She shut off her cell and moved forward, turned the corner and gazed into his dark eyes, feeling more full of life and emotion than she could ever remember feeling.

"I love it…" she whispered.

And you.

10

ANNABEL STOOD hardly daring to breathe. She had always imagined falling in love with someone would feel either of two ways. Either a moment of passionate blinding realization, a joyous radiant announcement with trumpets and floating hearts glistening like soap bubbles, popping and reforming in an endless ecstatic display, where birdies sang and the sun came out—complete with rainbow, of course—even if it was the middle of the night or the dead of winter.

Or an equally sudden and equally powerful but infinitely quiet moment. A gentle step marking the transition from knowing you weren't in love yet to the blissful certainty that you were. Like crossing an unmarked border and finding yourself in the same surroundings, yes, but in an entirely new country.

This was neither.

The minute her heart announced its new finding to her brain, her brain started the doubt machine whirring. No, no, no, she was feeling unusually vulnerable and therefore prone to romantic fantasy. By decorating her house, by taking her back to Hartland, Quinn had tapped into *her* inner need and made *her* feel wonderful and made *her* good memories resurface. All about *her*.

That wasn't love, that was ego, that was neediness, that was what-have-you-done-for-me-lately. Love went both ways. You took and you gave; you took to become a better, stronger person and you gave to make your partner better and stronger, too. She was mistaking infatuation for something deeper. And for crying out loud, she'd only been seeing him one week.

Quinn moved forward, put his hands on her shoulders, pulled her the rest of the way to him and kissed her, a long, slow exploring kiss that made a burn of excitement start in her chest and travel south to the hot, moist tropics. No question he was exciting to her. Physically. And mentally. And emotionally. But excitement fell in the infatuation camp. Part of the thrills that wouldn't last.

Though, granted, she'd been with plenty of men and never once thrilled like this. Not even close.

Quinn drew back, glowing candlelight reflected in his eyes, softening and romanticizing his features. He gave a tiny crooked smile and, without warning, the burn of excitement was lost to the painful swelling of her heart.

Infatuation. Still infatuation.

Okay, pretty damn serious infatuation. But she couldn't get carried away by…whatever was hell-bent on carrying her away. She had her business to think of. She had no room in her life for a long-term man. Linda and Evan had been right, she wasn't her mother; she couldn't be half of someone else, couldn't sacrifice herself and her goals for the sake of a man. She was whole and had to make her way alone, reach her goals by herself so she knew she could do it. Right? Right.

Annabel gave herself a mental kick in the rear. And? So? What was her point? She was fine. She knew the rules, knew her boundaries. She was infatuated with Quinn. He was here in her bedroom and for once they'd be able to spend quality time in good old-fashioned sheets instead of cars, couches or up against the wall.

These were good things. This was not time to panic and turn paranoid. When Quinn left, he left and she'd go on and conquer all that needed to be conquered.

She smiled at him, feeling balanced again, stronger, in control. Put her hands to his shoulders and sauntered forward, pushing him back to sit on the edge of the bed. She knelt between his legs, drew her hands seductively down the muscled surface of his chest and began undoing his shirt buttons.

One. Two. Three…oh, she liked what was emerging. The broad bulge of well-defined pectorals under soft cotton, mmm. One of her very favorite landscapes.

The last button gave. She pushed the material off his shoulders, following the path with caressing palms, and dragged the shirt down and off his powerful arms, right then left. The candles flickered around them. The music switched from traditional carols to mellow jazz arrangements. Annabel reached for the hem of his undershirt. Next to pectorals under cotton, the sight of a man's shoulder muscles bulging from a sleeveless undershirt came in a very close second, maybe even a dead heat. The combination was a total turn-on…as if she needed more of one than Quinn himself.

She pulled the undershirt up and over his head. He let her undress him, watched her all the while, the dark energy in his eyes belying his passivity. He might be giving her control now, but that look told her it was only a matter of time before he took it back.

Yes. Lots to look forward to.

She leaned forward to kiss his magnificent chest, rub her face against the coarse tickling hair, surprise him with a gentle bite to his nipple. Then moved downward, unsnapped his pants, unzipped, eased them and his briefs down while he lifted his lower body off the bed using the strength in his arms.

Yum.

The pants hit behind her where she tossed them; the snap made a metallic clank on her floor.

And then he was gloriously and totally naked in front of her, sitting on her bed. And she was fully clothed and in charge. She liked this. A lot.

See? If she still wanted to one-up him, it wasn't true love. Just the cozy fun of infatuation.

She tipped her head forward and let her hair caress his penis, slowly back and forth, moving in a dreamy rhythm. She wanted the night to build gradually. She wanted to give him so much pleasure, make him feel so wonderful that forever after in bed with other women, there would be no escaping thoughts of her.

Her head stopped moving until she made it continue. She resented the surge of jealousy at the thought of him with someone else. Quinn didn't belong to her. They were both here tonight because they chose to be. That was just right. That was enough.

She lifted her head suddenly so her hair flipped back behind her and she sent him a parted-lips look to tell him that what was next on her agenda involved her mouth and some of his most treasured anatomy.

His lips curved in a yes-please-go-ahead smile and she utterly ruined her fabulous sultry smoldering look of promise by smiling back in pure pleasure at the sight of him, so gorgeous and so glad to be here with her.

Of course, what naked man *wouldn't* be happy with a willing, openmouthed woman kneeling at his feet? But she couldn't help smiling back at him because, well, just because. He had that effect on her. It didn't mean anything.

Infatuation.

She lowered her lips to the head of his penis, felt it jump as she made the contact. Her lips opened wider, and she took him in bit by bit. Moistening him, warming him with her mouth, letting her tongue add to the pleasure her lips were giving by working it around his skin.

He tasted clean, male; she lifted off and bent down further, took his balls in her hand and nuzzled them, then let her tongue manipulate the small sacs inside.

His hands landed gently on her head, caressing her hair, not guiding her, letting her know he remembered she was attached to that mouth, thanking her for the pleasure. She smiled up at him again.

"Annabel." He whispered her name, touched her face, traced her eyebrows, her cheekbones, her lips.

She waited for more, but he just stroked her face gently with one finger, gazing at her as if nothing else in the world mattered.

And while kneeling at his feet, trying to be provocative and utterly sexual, something strange shifted in Annabel's heart. She felt all at once joyous and mournful; as if she wanted to get up and dance and maybe curl up and hide. Happy and sad; brave and scared to death.

Infatuation. Right?

"More?" She gave him a coy look and couldn't help grinning when he raised his eyebrows in a look that clearly said *Why on earth would I say no?*

She took him back in her mouth and settled into a rhythm, hands helping, wanting him to go out of his mind with how good it was.

But this time there was no thought of winning out over other women, and no more of wanting him to think she was the best he'd ever had. This time she just wanted him to feel wonderful because he'd made her feel wonderful so many times in so many ways.

Infatuation.

He moaned softly and she sped up the rhythm, turned on by his excitement even though she was the one giving. His hands found her hair again, urged her on in her rhythm without forcing. She sucked him avidly, eyes closed, passionately and insistently, bent on making him wild.

The first taste of his excitement registered in her mouth; the hands on her head slowed her rhythm, then stopped her. She lifted up slowly, then glanced questioningly at him from her knees.

"Stand up." He took her shoulders and half lifted her. "I want to undress you."

She stood in front of him, waiting for him to start, and became suddenly aware of her work-tired body, of the cooking smells that probably clung to her, of the stains on her clothes. "I didn't get to shower."

"Shh. You're fine. You're beautiful." He put his finger to her lips, then his warm hands slipped to her waist, raised her shirt, lifted it up and over her head, leaving her in her cotton camisole and bra. He ran his finger along the neckline of the camisole, the thin material nearly see-through. "One of these days I'd like to see you in this with no bra. Very sexy."

She nodded. "Yes. Okay."

As if she'd deny him anything right now. She'd never felt so nervous to be naked in front of a lover, like she was some virgin bride instead of the woman who had stripped off both clothes and inhibitions on camera. At the same time she was dying for the feel of his skin against hers, cheeks together, toes together and everything in between. Finally. After what seemed like weeks of wanting.

Off came the camisole, slid up and pulled over her head, then the tightening and release of the elastic around her chest and her bra joined it on the edge of a nearby chair. Her breasts hung free, tightening in response to the cool air and his nearness.

He brushed his thumbs around her areolas, over the nipples. Her breath caught coming in, then going out. Oh, it felt incredible. The way he touched her, unapologetic, confident, possessive, was as exciting as the sensations themselves. His hands swept lower, eased her black work pants down, then slid under her panties to caress her hips and lower the material off. She stepped out of both pants and panties eagerly with one foot, and lifted the other to let them slide off to the side.

There. Naked. Not knowing how to stand or where to put her arms—why was she being like this?

He caught her hands, lifted them to the side and over her head and stood there, with their arms forming an arc between them, gazing at her, her breasts thrust toward him by her slightly arched back, her stomach pulled flat by the same arch, the trimmed hair between her legs, then her legs themselves, all the way down to the floor.

"And?"

He looked at her curiously. "And what?"

"Do I pass inspection?"

He let go her hands and grabbed her up; she gave a silly squeal of surprise when he deposited her on the bed and loomed over her, grinning. "You are the most gorgeous woman I've ever seen."

She rolled her eyes, ridiculously pleased. "Right."

"I'm serious."

"You say that to all your women."

"Not to any of them. Stay here. I'll be right back." He lifted himself off the bed and left the room, his feet nearly soundless on her hardwood floors except for the one creaky board near the door.

Not to any of them? Was he serious? He couldn't be.

Oh, but she wanted him to be. Utterly, cross-his-heart serious.

The hall-closet door opened and closed; the water ran in her bathroom, then shut off. What was he doing? Annabel stretched on the smooth cotton of her sheets and stared at the ceiling, waiting to find out. The cool air in the room caressed her body. The music soothed her, and the candles sent shadows flickering on her walls. There wasn't anywhere in the world she'd rather be right now, no one she'd rather be with. The evening couldn't be more perfect.

Until the thought that her affair with Quinn would be over soon invaded her beautiful happiness and threatened to turn it butt-ugly. She wanted more nights like this with him. She wanted an unlimited supply, stretching ahead of her night after night forming a long row of nights, like a magic bridge spanning the rest of her...

Uh-oh.

Life?

The board near her door squeaked again. She swallowed her sudden panic and made herself smile genuine welcome at his return. "Hey."

"Miss me?"

"Terribly."

He sat next to her on the bed, tossed a pack of condoms onto the mattress and held up a wet washcloth and a towel. "Here's the shower you wanted."

She struggled up to her elbows and scowled playfully. "You are seriously spoiling me. Soon I'll start demanding jewels and large appliances, then villas and small countries."

"Someone needs to spoil you. You never do it."

"Oh? And who spoils you?"

He sent her a look. "The job is open."

"Do I need references?"

"No. You're hired." He cupped her chin playfully, then dropped his hand. "But it's your turn now. Lie back and relax. Close your eyes. You're going to like this."

"Yes, sir." She lay back and closed her eyes, not quite able to relax. He had the money to spoil himself any way he wanted to whenever he wanted to. She would have thought that was enough. Then the warm washcloth hit her left foot in a slow massaging motion, and she moaned in pleasure. On the other hand, there were some things money couldn't buy. Like having someone who cared about you, someone you were *infatuated* with, do the little everyday things that made life more than just a question of routine.

Quinn had no one to do those things for him. And in an unexpected wave of emotion that almost hurt, she wanted to be the one who could. Even for a while.

The washcloth traveled up higher, each slow, massaging stroke followed by the soft warmth of the towel, then the equally warm lips of Mr. Quinn Garrett, kissing her instep, her ankle, her knee, her lower thigh, her upper thigh…and oh darn, on to her fingers, just when she was gathering steam for the good stuff.

Each finger wet, massaged, dried, kissed, her forearm, upper arm, the process repeated on the other side. Then her shoulders, neck, her face, forehead, nose, lips washed, dried, kissed. She was losing her ability to breathe, caught between arousal and relaxation and the incredible tenderness of his actions, his attention to and reverence for her body's every part.

The washcloth trailed down, cool now, over her breasts. He must have lifted it then, because the edge swung back and forth on her skin until her nipples reached up like indignant sentinels under threat of attack. The air turned them chilly almost to where it was unpleasant, then the heat of his mouth made her eyes shoot open. She gasped and arched into the pressure.

"You like that?"

"Oh, yes."

"Mmm, me too." He moved to her other breast, traced the darker skin with his tongue, then bent and suckled again. Oh, she so loved that feeling, his warm, strong mouth on her cold, sensitive skin. She clutched his hair, lifted her hips, though there was nothing to push against—and why wasn't there? She was ready.

"Quinn."

"Mmm?"

"Can we—can you—"

"Shh. Be patient."

She groaned. Patient? She was going to die of horniness; you didn't talk patience in life-or-death matters.

The bath from heaven continued, slowly—way too slowly—down her stomach, her abdomen, just brushing the tip of her pelvis, then...

"Be right back."

Annabel moaned in frustration and heard him chuckle as he left the room. She smiled, lay waiting, eyes closed again, skin tingling from the alternating warm and cold and from his touch, anticipating his return and the washcloth between her legs—but mostly anticipating his return.

She was nuts about him. It was crazy.

He came back into the room. She kept her eyes closed, afraid that if she opened them she was going to beg him to stay in Milwaukee or take her back to California, give her a big wedding and lots of babies.

"Lift."

Her hips lifted. She felt a towel pushed under her, then his hands guided her back down.

"Spread for me, Annabel."

She obeyed his whispered command, opened her legs and felt the drip of hot water on her clitoris, trickling down her sex, caught by the towel under her. Then the washcloth was gently moving down and up, spreading her, cleaning her, arousing her like mad. Again the trickle of water. Again the slow slide of cloth on her sex.

She arched up into the sensation, breath coming harder, relaxation dissipating into the urgency of arousal.

Again the stream, the rubbing, then his touch stopped. She lay squirming slightly and felt his breath on her, blown through pursed lips, cooling her wet, heated sex.

Then the abrupt shift to warm as his open mouth joined to her, tongue probing, caressing, sending her to the edge of heaven.

But heaven like this wouldn't be enough, not tonight. She wanted them both to get there, if not exactly at the same time, then close. More than that, while their bodies engaged the physical, she wanted his face up here with her, his mouth to kiss, his words near her ears. She wanted him, wanted the emotions that she knew were going to come with the orgasms tonight.

This *was* infatuation, wasn't it?

She put her hands to his shoulders, tugged him up gently. He understood—didn't he always understand?— slid up beside her, grabbed the condom and put it on while she stroked his arm, his back, unable to stop touching him. He was so beautiful, so male, so perfectly stunning in the soft candlelight.

"Annabel."

"Mmm?"

He moved over her and stopped, knees between her legs, hands on either side of her head, watching her intently. "I want to make love to you."

She swallowed sudden fear. Why was she scared? This was what she wanted, too. "Yes."

"Not screw, not fuck, make love. Do you understand?"

A tear found the corner of her eye and spilled over onto her cheek. "Yes."

"Is that what you want, too?"

She looked into his eyes, trying her damnedest not to start sobbing, and nodded.

"Good." He smiled then, leaned down and kissed her mouth so tenderly she started to cry in earnest.

"Uh…Annabel?" He drew back and stared at her in concern. "Is this a truly miserable moment for you?"

Laughter mixed in with her tears, then took over completely.

"I'm sorry," she gasped. "I'm a total case. I'm sorry."

He waited, smiling, until her weird hysteria spent itself. "It's okay. I think I know what you mean."

"What." A stray giggle burst out. "I wish you'd tell me, because I am so confused by how I feel, I haven't a clue."

"No? Let me explain." He brushed hair back from her forehead, then bent and kissed her again. "Like this."

Her giggles died; she wrapped her arms around his neck and kissed him back as if she was being handed her last chance to kiss a man for the rest of her life. No, more than that. So much more than that. As if it was her last chance to kiss Quinn.

The kiss turned openmouthed, hot, passionate. He lowered himself onto her; she opened and lifted to welcome him in.

He slid inside and began to move, filling her body, filling her heart.

She wanted to cry out even before her body was ready to come. She wanted him to move harder, and she wanted him to stay gentle. She wanted it to last forever, this hot stroking of their bodies, the push-pull excitement of his erection slowly thrusting and receding inside her. He lowered his head next to hers, cheek pressed to her cheek, slid his arms under her to gather her closer still, and rode gently, reverently, hugging her to him as if she was part of him.

I love you.

The words bubbled up from deep inside her, came shooting into her consciousness. *I love you.* She shook her head next to him, her forehead bumping his temple. She couldn't love him. She'd be lost, swallowed up, obliterated. Her life would take a completely different turn now that she'd finally found the path she really, really wanted to take.

"What is it?"

She screwed her eyes shut, ashamed that she wasn't brave enough to share what she was feeling. "It's…so good."

"*We're* so good."

"Yes." She opened her eyes and looked into his. "We are."

His thrusting went off rhythm; his eyes darkened. Then he bent to kiss her, kissed her again, brought his arms out from under her, braced them on either side of her head, and thrust faster and with an element of mastery and ownership that unexpectedly drove her wild, unearthed some secret dark desire to be dominated.

She pressed herself up against him, clasped his smooth muscled back close, closer, panting, emitting occasional cries like a wounded animal but feeling no pain, only the hot pleasure of their joining. And slowly, surely, amid the emotional turmoil and the arousal, something took over inside her, left her conscious self in the dust. Her body started striving for its completion; she opened her legs wider, brought her knees to her shoulders. He made a guttural sound and drove still harder. His lips found hers and he kissed her ravenously, tongue inside her mouth, now plunging to echo the movements of his hips, now circling hers. She wrapped her legs across his back, submitted completely, letting him move, letting him carry her closer…closer… the kiss pushing her over the edge that rushed inevitably toward her.

I love you.

She tensed, terrified she'd said the words out loud at the same time her orgasm swept her, burned its path upward, then receded into the pulsing contractions, the gradual decline of intense sensation.

Quinn's thrusting quickened further. "Am I hurting you?"

"No."

"Sure?" he panted.

"Yes. It's fabulous," she whispered. "I love it hard."

He let out a low groan, three more thrusts and she felt his body tense into his own climax. A responding thrill shot through her. Her words had pushed him over, and she loved that he responded so perfectly to what she said and what she felt.

Quinn lay quiet on top of her, breathing long, grateful breaths. She skimmed her hands over his back, his buttocks, his shoulders, still shocked by the intensity with which those three little words had insisted on being spoken out loud.

Thank goodness, she hadn't; Quinn would have

freaked. She shouldn't even be thinking them. There was no way she could be in love in such a short time. If the words had come out, she'd have ruined everything, complicated her life to a degree that would take weeks if not months, if not a lifetime to uncomplicate.

He lifted his head and smiled, kissed her forehead, cheeks and chin. "Good?"

"The best." She smiled back, hoping she looked peaceful and fulfilled and not tormented like hell with feelings she couldn't sort out.

He rolled to one side, keeping their bodies attached, raised her leg so he could slip one of his in between hers. Then he started moving again, very slowly, gently, eyes closed, hand trailing down her thigh, body arched away from hers to keep a comfortable angle.

She reached out and touched his chest, traced the now-damp curls of hair, looked down and watched the thick base of his erection appearing and disappearing inside her, arousal at a low, comfortable simmer. She could probably go all night with this man, all week. She hoped he'd never stop. Because once he left her body, he'd leave her house, too.

As if he'd heard her, he opened his eyes, gradually slowed his thrusting, then touched her cheek, pulled out, got up and disposed of the condom. He blew out the candles then stayed at the window looking out.

Annabel stiffened, throat miserably tight, waiting for him to turn on the light, already hating the shock of the coming brightness, knowing he'd leave, knowing it would hurt this time way more than it ever had. She'd had great sex before, but this had gone far beyond great sex into the land of the emotional, and left her raw and vulnerable in a way she hadn't experienced before and didn't much like.

If only he wouldn't leave tonight.

"Can you stay?" She whispered the words into the welcome darkness, thankful for its cover. No way would she be able to hide her pain if he said no.

"Yes. I'd like to."

Her breath came out on a small laugh of delight.

"What's funny?"

"Not funny. Happy. What are you watching out there?"

"The moon. It's a tiny crescent, sharp like a piece of glass. And there's a real thaw on, water dripping even at this hour."

"It was pretty slushy driving back." She smiled at his broad, spreading shoulders silhouetted against the window by the light from the streetlamp outside. She felt relaxed, warm, utterly content discussing the weather with the man who had made love to her mind as well as her body and who was going to stay all night and probably do it again. It felt cozy and domestic and in some weird sense, as if she'd finally grown up enough to have a boyfriend, not just a lover.

Quinn drew the shades and shut the curtains over them. "Quite a snowman across the street, I noticed it earlier."

"Mmm. Kid and his mom across the street did it."

"Frosty?" He slid back into bed and pulled her close.

"Brunnhilde."

He laughed. She moved closer to his warmth, wrapped her legs around his, put her hand to his chest enjoying the vibrations of his laughter, enjoying the feel of his skin, enjoying him. She hadn't lain like this with a man since…ever. Not for more than a minute or two. So she wouldn't get any sleep tonight. And she'd be a zombie in the morning cooking for his party. Right now, who cared? It was delicious. Deliciously warm, deliciously silent.

Until Quinn cleared his throat and in a rich baritone, did the last thing she'd expect him to do: started singing "Frosty the Snowman." She giggled at first, and then when it became apparent he intended to keep singing, she listened incredulously, then with real enjoyment. He sang pretty well for a computer geek, and she had to admit she was charmed.

"'So he said let's run and have some fun, now before I melt away…'" His voice trailed off in the darkness.

The meaning of his words sank in and Annabel's smile faded. "Is that what we're doing?"

"You tell me."

She nudged him playfully. "You first."

He chuckled. "Ah, no, we control freaks won't risk owning up to our feelings, will we?"

"What a surprise."

"Okay, I'll go first." He turned and cleared his throat. "You ready?"

"Yes."

"You sure?"

"Positive."

"Really sure?"

"Sta-a-l-ling…"

"Guilty." His hand stroked her shoulder; she felt the tension rise in his body.

Immediately a strong urge rose to put her feelings out

there first, spare him any tension or fear, make it safe for him.

"I'm not ready for this to end."

"Will you come to California to visit me?"

They spoke at the same time and laughed together, nervously. Annabel bit her lip. "I would love to come to California, I just don't see how I can—"

"Take the time?"

She inhaled deeply, blew out in a sigh. "Predictable, huh."

"Like a clock. How did you get that way?"

"Gee, Freud, I dunno."

"You must have some idea."

"I do, I do." She lifted her hand, let it drop back onto his chest. "I suppose I'm following in my father's no-nonsense footsteps. Or rather taking up the challenge he laid down that being a girl, I couldn't. Or maybe fulfilling the success he denied my mother."

"You think she regretted giving up her career?"

"How could she not?"

He shrugged. "Granted, I came to your family from a skewed perspective, but I've never seen a couple as happy as your parents."

Annabel lifted her head. "So that means I'm uptight and driven for no reason whatsoever?"

He grinned, giving her an affectionate squeeze. "We'll work on you. Not that I'm exactly Mr. Spontaneity."

"No." She shifted beside him, wondering about her mom, loving that he said "we" and wanting to tell him she thought they were good for each other, that he'd already started changing her for the better, and that she wanted to help him, too. But she was too pathetically scared it would sound as though she was picking out their furniture already, and maybe too scared she would find herself wanting to. "So what's your life like in California?"

"When I'm not traveling? Let's see. I get up every morning at five, work out, am at the office by eight, sit in meetings, put out fires, read too many reports, write too many letters, take someone dull out to lunch, do it again in the afternoon, and in the evening I either speak to business groups, have dinner with a friend or go home and read."

"Wow."

"More glamorous than you ever thought possible, right?"

"Way more." She smiled even as she felt the fear building in her at the question she wanted so much to ask him. "How long can you stay?"

"Tonight or in Milwaukee?"

"Both."

"I'm not leaving here until you kick me out." He brought his hand up to lie across his forehead. "And I'm going to Maine on Christmas Eve, then home to California."

"Tomorrow." Annabel swallowed against the stab of pain. Not a surprise. She knew he'd be leaving. "Your mom will be glad to see you."

"I'll be glad to see her, too."

She stroked his chest, down his stomach, back up again, loving the warm, alive feel of him next to her. "What's her name?"

"Bridget. It means 'resolute strength,' which fits her. What does Annabel mean?"

She rolled her eyes. "Graceful beauty."

"Let me check." He rolled to the side and relit a candle beside her bed, then slid back beside her, took hold of her chin and inspected her like an auto mechanic checking a newly arrived part. "Yup. Graceful beauty it is."

She snorted and pushed his hand away. "What does Quinn mean?"

"'Wise.' And Garrett means, 'with a mighty spear.'"

Annabel burst out laughing. "As one who was just speared, I can testify that it is indeed mighty."

"Why thank you." He cupped the back of her head and kissed her mouth, then again, as if the one time wasn't nearly enough. Which in her opinion it damn well wasn't.

"So, Mr. Mighty Spear…"

"Mmm?"

"You said I'd know when the time was right to ask about your family."

"Yes, I did."

"I'm guessing now."

"Okay." He rolled onto his back, dark eyes staring at the ceiling, lashes and candlelight making wavering shadows on his cheeks. "Here's the fun version. Dad was an alcoholic, often violent. Mom protected me as best she could, but he got to me too sometimes. When I left for college, Mom kicked him out. He found someone else to beat up and eventually drank himself to death. I was an odd kid, a loner, not many friends. And they all lived happily ever after. The end."

"Oh, my God, Quinn." She thought of him as the teenager who'd shown up at their house that fall— quiet, aloof, wary, and her heart felt as if it would break retroactively.

"That year with your family was like paradise. That's why I remember so much of it."

"I can see why." Her eyes filled with tears, she couldn't help it. It was as if his pain was happening to her.

"I spoke to Mom yesterday. She said when I came home from that year I talked about you incessantly." He turned to her, eyebrows lifted, eyes watchful. "What do you think *that* means?"

She smiled through her tears at his teasing tone. "Um, that you've been in love with me your entire life?"

She meant the words to come out flippantly, said with a smile, teasing him back. But her throat was still thick from emotion and the sentence came out deadly serious, throaty and passionate. *Oh, God.* She wanted to crawl under the bed and live forever after with the dust bunnies. *What* had possessed her to say that?

"Quinn." She struggled up onto one elbow and forced herself to grin wickedly. "I was kidding. Don't freak out."

He put a hand to her hair and brushed it back from her face with such tenderness, her wicked grin didn't have a chance of survival.

"I didn't freak out, Annabel." He lifted his head and kissed her. "I was actually wondering the same thing."

11

ANNABEL HALF WOKE to the vague feeling that it was late and she had huge things to do and not nearly enough time to do them in. Of course she woke up feeling that way every day, but something was different this morning.

Her body registered the heat of another body against her back. *Oh* my. She'd spent the entire night with Quinn and actually slept. She could never sleep with anyone in the bed. The few times she'd tried were such exercises in restless, blanket-warring, snore-blocking insomniac frustration, she'd finally put her foot down and wouldn't let anyone stay.

But here he was, and here she was, and it was morning, though probably pretty early. She blinked completely awake and lifted on her elbows, looked at the clock and gasped. Eight o'clock, how could it be? She hadn't woken up once, not once! Slept like the dead with a man beside her…with *Quinn* in her bed…how on earth did she do that?

"H'lo." A strong arm looped itself around her and brought her back to lie against a warm chest.

"Good morning." She tried to remember her menu for the dinner party at his apartment tonight. How badly off was she? Stefanie would be here at nine. If she got up now and managed to—

"Sleep well?" The hand attached to said strong arm began to investigate her breasts, her stomach, and… mmm…so on.

"Quinn." She tried to move away, but it was like trying to push through a metal subway turnstile without having paid. "It's eight already."

"So?" His fingers reached their intended goal between her legs and she grabbed his hand away, trying not to savor the warmth of his body pressed against her back.

"*So*…I can't believe I overslept. I have to get up and start on your dinner party. I haven't shopped yet for the perishable stuff, I need to—"

"Get takeout." He moved quickly, flipped her on her back, pinned her there and began kissing her stomach, moving downward, obviously intending to be on his way to making her a happy, happy woman.

Except this wasn't the time for happiness. This was the time for work. "I can't do this. I have to make a phyllo mushroom tart and salad, roast a leg of lamb with potatoes, olives and artichokes, and prepare raspberry gelato, raspberry chocolate tartlets with hazelnut crusts and miniature raspberry parfaits."

"So what's your point?" His tongue prepared to invade her body and her sanity. She wiggled free and sat up on the bed, eyeing him warily.

"I have to get going. I can't stay. This party is important. I want to do it right for you."

"I don't mind. And I can help again if you want. Or why not just make one dessert instead of three?"

"You don't understand. You're—"

"Leaving tomorrow morning."

Ouch. Okay. That shut her up. Annabel dropped her eyes to the sheet, not able to meet his gaze. "True."

"And that's it for us."

"It is?" She did look at him then, anxiously, she was sure. A miserable little balloon started inflating in her chest, taking up too much room and hurting.

"Apparently. I don't live here, you said you can't come to California even to visit. Where does that leave us?"

"Apart." She whispered the words while the balloon inflated further, to bursting point, only she had a feeling this balloon would never pop, just keep growing larger and larger and hurting more and more.

"Right. Apart. So I want to make love to you this morning. Cut out one of the desserts. Buy prepackaged greens for the salad. Better yet, get a bucket of chicken with sides, call it a dinner party and spend the whole damn day with me, Annabel."

Her heart reacted viscerally to the emotion in his voice while her head knew it was impossible. "I can't do that. You've got the bigwig from Janson Corp. coming. This is my job. My reputation. Would you show up to a big speaking engagement unprepared? Give the audience an aural bucket of chicken when they were expecting three courses of perfection?"

"Touché." He sighed and scrubbed his hand through his hair. "No. I wouldn't."

"I won't, either."

"I know." He took her face in his hands and kissed her forehead, a long, sweet kiss that for all its chasteness turned her gooey and hot. "Forget I suggested it. Pure selfish greed."

"Yep." She sent him a sly glance. "Although…I *could* just make the raspberry tarts and the parfait."

"*Now* we're talking." He reached for her waist, pulled her forward, then eased her onto her back and lay over her, reached for a condom from her bedside table. "You're *sure* you can't serve fast food?"

"I'm sure." She put her arms around his neck and moved her hips suggestively. "But why don't you try and convince me otherwise?"

"Deal."

Half an hour later, they lay together, panting subsided into slow, relaxed breaths, and mmm, Annabel was practically sore from being convinced. He was the best convincer she'd had in a long, long time. No, ever. She'd miss him like mad when he left. And that was such an atrocious understatement she couldn't believe she'd even thought it.

Last night he'd shocked her by wondering out loud if the *L* word applied and she'd started bawling again, oh, my God, what a wreck she was. Annabel, the great implacable one, who ran her business on her own, weathered the storms, out there every day upbeat and positive—she'd been reduced to a hormonal sniffling wreck.

If this was love, well, frankly, this felt more like insanity.

What had there been to say? No more than had been said this morning. In the context of their lives, whether or not they were in love didn't make a whole hell of a lot of difference either way.

Quinn lifted his head from next to hers, glanced over at the clock and back with a raised eyebrow. "I suppose round two is out of the question?"

She didn't need to know the time to answer that one. "Uh-huh."

"You sure?" He moved in and out of her, not fully erect, but still hard enough to make her squirm and wish she could change her mind. "Maybe you could only make one dessert?"

"Hmm." She giggled. "I suppose I *could* make just one big raspberry tart and serve it with whipped cream."

"Have I ever told you how much—" His cell phone rang. He scowled and lifted off her, carefully pulling out so not to hurt her or disturb the condom. "Sorry. Annoying as hell I know, but I have to take calls after eight."

"I understand." Business, she understood. Matters of the heart were completely mysterious.

"Hello?" He sat on the edge of the bed. She moved closer and spooned around him, unable to resist even the smallest chance to touch him.

She should just be honest and face it. She didn't want to cook at all. She wanted to lie here with him for the rest of the day, for the rest of the week, for the rest of the year and beyond. Talk, laugh, make love, eat only when necessary. Was this what her mother had felt? Was this why she'd given up a shot at courtroom fame? And was Quinn right, that Mom had found the trade-off well worth it?

For the first time in her life, she could imagine how that might be true. Her mom might even have said so, in so many ways, but Annabel hadn't been ready to hear it. Maybe Annabel was in love. Or maybe she was just growing up and figuring out that things were never quite as black-and-white as they seemed in youth.

She drew her hand down the wonderful muscled back

next to her. Maybe she could just bake the potatoes plain, in with the lamb. And serve olives in a dish on the side. They were perfectly delicious on their own. Artichokes were out of season now anyway.

"Okay, yes. I'm delighted you'll be there, thanks very much for calling." He snapped off the phone, then tipped his head back as if he was asking the ceiling for guidance on a troubling issue.

"What is it?" She let her finger ski down the vertebrae moguls of his spine, down to the sexy hollow just above his buttocks. "Extra people tonight? Back to two desserts?"

"Two more people." He twisted around so he could see her face. His own looked fairly grim. "Something tells me you're really not going to be happy with a bucket of chicken now."

"Oh?" Alarm bells started ringing. Loudly. "Why's that?"

"That call? The guests coming tonight?"

"Ye-e-es?"

"I wasn't sure if he'd make it, so I didn't want to get your hopes up."

Annabel lifted her head off the mattress. "What do you mean? Who is it?"

He chuckled with dry irony and let his hand drop down on her rear with a playful smack. "Time to get up, Ms. Personal Chef. Tonight you're cooking for Adolph Fox."

ANNABEL CALLED goodbye through her back door to poor, exhausted Stefanie, thanked her for the morning and early afternoon of frantic help, then hoisted the last bag of food into her minivan to take over to Quinn's apartment. Adolph Fox would be there. She couldn't quite wrap her brain around the fact. That must explain why she wasn't more pumped up. Something had to explain it. For heaven's sake, this man was her idol. At worst, he could give her valuable advice, at best become her mentor and launch her on her way to the big-time career she'd always wanted.

Maybe she was tired. Maybe she had some Quinn-induced block to actually understanding what this could mean to her.

Maybe she was so crazy about him that she couldn't bring herself to care.

She slammed the liftgate down. Which was exactly why she'd wanted so badly to keep her heart free. Now that Quinn had wormed his way in, her goals were fuzzing out. She couldn't think past the next time she'd get to see him, couldn't stop trying to scheme how she could find some way to keep seeing him after he left tomorrow.

Was she turning into her mother? She couldn't imagine being happy just as Mrs. Quinn Garrett. Couldn't imagine a lifetime wondering how far she could have taken her company and her talent and her name.

And yet Quinn had been back in her life a week—granted an intense week—and already the thought of seeing him only the odd times he managed to make it back to Milwaukee didn't feel as if it was going to be enough.

Not nearly.

She closed her back door and rested her head against the cool glass window for just a second. To regroup. As if one second resting her head against cool glass was going to solve anything. But rushing to this dinner party, where she'd be caught between Quinn hosting and Adolph Fox guesting, was going to be much more symbolic pressure than she was in the mood for.

What was she in the mood for?

Quinn.

Lying next to him. Cooking with him in the kitchen. Laughing, kissing, flirting like a stupid, giggling adolescent head case.

It was heaven. And she'd been away from heaven for a very long time. She hadn't felt this connected to someone since her mom had died. She loved her brother John, she was close to him, but he had his own family and rarely came home to visit.

Okay, maybe that was partly her fault for not being more accessible. She should invite him to come up sometime.

Either way, she really needed to get going.

"Annabel."

Annabel yanked her head back from the glass and turned to send neighbor Kathy an embarrassed smile. "Hi."

"Are you okay?" Kathy's plump face was creased with worry.

"Yes. Fine." Annabel smiled harder, touched that Kathy seemed so concerned about a woman who regularly avoided her. "Just gathering my thoughts before I go."

"Oh. Okay." She didn't look convinced, but thank goodness was too polite to pry. "Jackson said you came by to say hello to Brunnhilde."

"Oh. Yes." Annabel tried not to look impatient. For once she wasn't being people-phobic, she really had to leave.

"Of course she's not quite so glorious anymore with this melt. But anyway, Jackson said I should invite you to lunch sometime." She smiled tenderly at the mention of her son. "You made quite a conquest."

"Oh. Well. That would be...nice." Annabel laughed. She'd accepted to be polite, but was surprised to find herself thinking that lunch with Kathy might actually *be* nice. A break from her workday. Someone new to talk to after Quinn left.

"Did you hear what happened to Mr. Bailey?"

"No." Uh-oh. Gossip coming. Annabel resisted the urge to do two things: check her watch and ask who the hell Mr. Bailey was.

"He came down with a horrible flu and bronchitis. So now we're going to have the party Christmas Eve at my house. It will be sort of cramped, my place isn't as big as his, and he was going to provide the turkey, so we'll have to do without that, but it will be fun, still." She looked hopefully at Annabel. "Lots of good people on this block."

Annabel sighed. She had no desire to go to the party—until a picture came of her sitting alone in her house with Quinn in Maine. "Maybe I'll stop by, thanks."

"Oh that would be great." Kathy clapped her hands. "Well, I see you're on your way somewhere, and I'd better get back to cleaning and make sure Jackson hasn't torn the house apart."

"Okay." Annabel gave a friendly wave, trying not to rush to her car too obviously. But chatting was one thing she didn't have time for. She and Quinn and Stefanie, bless her, had managed to do a great deal of prep work, but there was still a lot left to do.

She jumped into her van and drove just this side of recklessly over to Quinn's apartment on Prospect Street near the lake. She parked, got out and opened the liftgate to unload. Perishables first—she'd put them in the bag on the right with the—

Arms slid around her waist. "Your manservant awaits."

Annabel started, then turned, her heart going into triple-time rhythm—just because it was Quinn, not because he'd startled her. "How is it that you anticipate my every need?"

"Because we're cosmically in tune with each other on every level."

Annabel lifted an eyebrow.

He grinned. "That and I was watching for you from the lobby."

"Thanks." She took the time to trace his lips with her finger, because it seemed incredibly important to do just then. "You smile a lot more now than when I first met you."

"And why do you think that is?"

"Um…you're happier?"

"And why do you think *that* is?"

She shrugged and blushed. "Me?"

"You," he whispered, and kissed her. "Tomorrow isn't going to be the end, Annabel. We'll find a way."

She nodded, suddenly too thick throated to trust herself to speak. With every part of her being, she suddenly wanted that to be true. Wanted to dump her groceries and Adolph Fox into Lake Michigan and be swept off to…to…

To what? Sit around and clean house for him? Hell,

he didn't even need someone to clean his house. He could afford one person for each room.

She needed her career, and her career was here. She'd invested too much into Milwaukee to pick up stakes and move because she'd gone off the deep end over a man for a week. Whatever way they found to be together would have to include Chefs Tonight.

"Help me unload?" She pulled him down by his jacket collar and kissed him.

"That's what I'm here for."

They unloaded the van, brought the groceries and dishes in various states of completion upstairs to his apartment, where he'd set a beautiful table for six, a low, cascading floral arrangement in the center with red-berried holly and white freesia.

Annabel got the leg of lamb into the oven and for the next two hours they worked companionably together, preparing the meal, setting out the hors d'oeuvres to have with drinks beforehand.

They didn't speak much, intent on working, but Annabel sensed another tension. Neither of them wanted the next day to come. For all Quinn's assurances, neither of them could really see a solution to how they could end up together in any way that made sense or would keep their relationship thriving.

She poured cashews into an olive-wood bowl and forced herself to concentrate. Adolph Fox was coming—earlier than the other couple who'd called to say they'd be late—and she wanted to make the best impression possible. That was the main thing tonight. She couldn't lose track of that.

Finally, at five forty-five, she showered and dressed

in Quinn's room, looking longingly at his bed, imagining them both in it later, spending a last lazy night together. She felt a strange push-pull about the evening, wanting it over as much as she wanted it to happen.

Makeup on, panty hose, low heels, a black dress with red roses. She was just fussing the last fuss with her hair when the doorbell announced the arrival of Adolph Fox.

She took her place at Quinn's side, hostess for the evening as well as cook. For a second, she had a strange, disorienting flashback to her parents greeting arriving guests, and wondered if they'd taken this kind of pride in their planned evening and in each other.

"Ready?" Quinn smiled at her, hand on the doorknob, and she nodded, her heart pounding for once over something other than the fact that he looked like a Greek god.

"Let 'er rip."

He opened the door and there stood her hero, tall, handsome in a light gray suit with a silver tie, the man who had his picture in every freezer section in America.

Except clearly the picture was several years old. Or decades.

"Mr. Fox, nice to see you." Quinn shook his hand and gestured in. "Mrs. Fox, you look wonderful. This is Annabel Brightman, your hostess and chef for the evening."

"Ahh." Adolph Fox shook her hand, and kept holding it, eyeing her with his baby blues as if she were Grade A prime on sale for half price. "*Enchanté* as they say in France, delighted to meet you, Ms. Brightman."

"Annabel, please." She smiled graciously and attempted to disengage her hand in order to greet Mrs. Fox, but apparently Adolph felt that was unnecessary.

"And you must call me Dolph." He smiled, showing

teeth so blindingly white and perfect she suspected dentist interference.

He really needed to let go of her hand, because his poor wife was still standing in the doorway while Quinn put their coats away, and Annabel hadn't had the chance to say hello.

"So Quinn tells me you're a talented personal chef, eh, Annabel? Trying to carve out a niche for yourself?"

"I'm off to a good start, sir." The title her father had insisted they use slipped out before she could stop herself.

"Uh-uh-uh, Dolph." He waggled a scolding finger, then tucked her hand under his arm and dragged her into Quinn's living room, but not before Annabel shot Quinn a look and registered his amusement.

Fine, be that way. She took a deep breath and prepared herself for what was undoubtedly going to be a long evening. Her last with Quinn, at least this time around. And instead of spending it writhing in the sheets with him, she'd be pandering to this man who deserved a lot more respect than she was summoning for him at the moment. Not to mention that she owed Quinn a lot for setting this evening up.

"So, tell me about Annabel." Adolph sank into the large green-gray wing chair, tented his fingers under his lips, crossed his long legs and appeared to be all ears.

Quinn escorted in Adolph's wife whose name Annabel would apparently have to figure out at some point later in the evening, gestured her onto the dark blue sofa with silk-embroidered pillows and disappeared into the kitchen, ostensibly to pour drinks. Clearly he was trying to give Annabel as much time with her mentor as possible. And as grateful as she should be for the chance to talk to Mr. Fox, she kept glancing at the doorway of the kitchen to see when Quinn would come back.

Again, past images of her parents rose up—Mom entertaining guests, introducing them to each other and to appropriate conversation topics, while Dad manned the bar. Again she got that eerie sense that she'd grown up, gone beyond her childhood into a future like her parents, and that it fit her easily and comfortably. Whatever the hell that meant, she didn't want to know. Not now, not tonight, with her dream career personified in front of her.

She smiled at Mr. Fox—Dolph—and launched into a description of Chefs Tonight, how she'd started with one customer, the friend of a friend, and grown to ten regular families. She described the special programs she had in place, and the ones she was thinking of starting next year around more holidays—egg hunts at Easter, July Fourth picnics at the fireworks. "And then someday, I would like to have a mail-order business nationwide, with entrées prepared here and sent out, or…" She smiled, gestured to him.

Dolph chuckled. "You want to be me."

"I wouldn't mind."

"Good." He accepted a Kir Royale from a tray Quinn offered. "I like to hear that. But you should know the road is a tough, long one and there are lots of sacrifices."

"I'm not afraid of hard work." She jumped to her feet and passed around the tray of blue corn chips spread with taramasalata, her own recipe and combination.

"It's more than hard work. My first marriage fell apart. And my second. And my third. Now I'm back with old Delia here, my first."

Annabel nearly tipped the hors d'oeuvres out on the carpet. If "Old Delia" was uncomfortable she didn't show it, but then most likely the surgeon's knife had rendered her unable to move her face.

"I not only lost marriages, I lost friendships on the way up." Adolph grabbed a chip off her tray. "Made dozens of enemies."

"And you barely know our children."

Adolph ignored his wife's bitter comment and crunched the chip. His face spread into a smile. "Ingenious combination. Very good."

"Thank you." Annabel's pleasure at his compliment was tempered by dismay at the portrait of his personal isolation.

"Humph. He's a lonely old fart is what he is." Delia handed her glass to Quinn, who registered a flash of surprise that it was empty before he got up to refill it.

Annabel sat again and picked up her own glass, which had been depleted by all of a sip. Uh-oh. Husband neglectful. Wife drinking. Not a pretty picture. "So, Mr.— Dolph—do you regret what you've accomplished?"

"Nonsense." He lifted his glass in a toast; Delia rolled her eyes as if she'd not only heard what was about to come out of his mouth a hundred times, but had suffered during ninety-nine of them. "I am Adolph Fox. I promise fresh, honest ingredients at an affordable price. I didn't get where I am today by faking it."

Annabel started feeling more than a little uncomfortable. Looked to her like he was left only with his vanity. Vanity and a wife who thought he was an old fart. And money. And his picture on every box in the store, and hundreds of thousands of households in the U.S. eating his food.

Quinn walked back into the room carrying Delia's new drink, sat next to her and met Annabel's gaze. Even across the room, the pull to him was so strong, she could barely breathe. She found herself nodding automatically as Dolph started in on a long, overdetailed story of his beginnings. Only a small part of her sent warning signals that this was information she had been eagerly looking forward to hearing. The rest of her had gone off on a daydream. Wondering how she could take time away from the business, manage to fly to California here and there, maybe even have a couple of weeks off. After Easter and before wedding season might be possible. She had plans for simple post-wedding brunches to feed lingering out-of-town guests and relieve harried moms and dads of the happy couple who had hosted one too many meals.

How much of it would she give up for this man?

The doorbell announced the cheerful, chatty Fussells—she tall and thin, he short and round—who burst in with apologies for being late, politely declined a predinner drink and were ushered by Annabel and Quinn to the table along with Adolph and a wobbly Delia.

The question lingered in Annabel's mind throughout the meal, which she was thrilled came out perfectly. The lamb was cooked just right; the courses arrived at a proper pace at proper temperatures; the wines Quinn chose complemented the food perfectly. Adolph ate with relish, praising the food, the ambiance, the table. And more and more as the meal wound down, as they went back to the living room for coffee and cognac and

Valrhona chocolate, he'd lapse into silence, studying Annabel speculatively until she was going nuts wanting to ask what the heck he was thinking.

Finally, after yet another European vacation story by the Fussells, a telling silence hit and the Fussells made their excuses and left, heaping praise on Annabel and promising to hire her for their next event.

Back in the living room, the party essentially over and her precious time with Quinn ticking away, Annabel was dismayed that Mr. and Mrs. Fox showed no signs of leaving. Adolph requested another cognac. Delia closed her eyes and slid gracefully sideways to snore, openmouthed on the couch.

"And she wonders why I have mistresses." Adolph spoke with contempt, which made Annabel wince. She tried to imagine Adolph and Delia young and falling in love. Imagined her parents and what they had together. What made the difference? Luck? Maturity? Had Adolph's career contributed as much as Delia seemed to think?

"So." Adolph put his drink on the table beside his chair. "Now that we're alone, on to the more important things. Annabel, I'm getting old. My advisors are telling me I need youth in my company, a younger image."

He paused and sipped his espresso; the cup looked tiny and too dainty in his large hands. Annabel's heart started to pound. She glanced at Quinn, who'd moved himself out of drool-reach of Delia and was watching Annabel intently with an expression she couldn't read.

"I want someone presentable to be a co-representative to the public, but who knows her way around a kitchen. No faking it in my company. Do you know what I mean?"

"Yes, I do." She tried to say the words in a clear voice, but they came out croaky. Was what she thought was about to happen really about to happen? Her cheeks felt hot; her eyes saw the room slightly indistinctly.

"I didn't want a big-name chef or a rising star, I want someone who will carry the stamp of Adolph Fox."

Annabel nodded, too overwhelmed even to speak.

"Quinn and I met at some charity fund-raiser or other, what was that, Quinn?"

"American Heart Association." He spoke still looking at Annabel.

"Yes, right, that was it. Memory like a sieve these days. Anyway, he called when he heard I'd be in town and mentioned you, and you sounded like you had the right stuff. I asked him to set up this little dinner party and I'm delighted I did."

She smiled graciously, mind whirling. Was she crazy, or was she about to get everything she'd ever wanted handed to her on a silver tray she wouldn't even have to wash afterward?

"So." Adolph Fox put his cup down, leaned back in the chair and crossed his hands over his belly. "How would you, Annabel Brightman, like to be the very first Adolph Fox Girl?"

12

THE SECOND THE DOOR CLOSED behind Dolph's broad back and Delia's round tottering one, Annabel cut loose.

"Oh, my gosh!" She put her hands to her face, took them off to stare at Quinn, then let out a burst of slightly hysterical laughter. "I can't believe it."

"Believe it." He smiled, hands to his hips pushing back his jacket. "Pretty amazing, Fox Girl."

"Ew." She wrinkled her nose. "I hate the title. But I'm sure that won't show up on the products. Just my picture and my signature, as he said."

A huge burst of adrenaline shot through her and she did an absolutely appalling version of a pirouette. "My picture! My signature! This is so huge! This is so amazing! Everything I've wanted just like that."

"In one swell foop as your mom used to say."

Her appalling pirouette came to a merciful end. "Mom would have been so proud of me. And Dad, ha! He'd be eating his shorts. His own daughter, who happens to be a *woman,* making it this far. Ha!"

"He'd be proud of you, too."

"I know." She floated her way over to Quinn and took hold of his jacket lapels. "He would have been, deep down. Though it also would have made him a little cranky."

"You think?" He covered her hands tenderly with his, but something about the way his words came out and the way his eyes had lost some of their earlier warmth made her joy sit up and get nervous.

"I have you to thank for all this, Quinn. Don't think I don't realize that."

"You don't have to thank me. You're right for the job or Adolph wouldn't have offered it to you."

"Uh-uh-uh, please." She waggled her finger in a shameless caricature. "Call him Dolph."

"Yes, yes, of course." He caressed her hands, wrists, lower arms. "The Dolphster."

"And his lovely 'old' wife." Annabel moved closer to Quinn and tilted her head up at him. "Did she say more than two words the entire evening?"

"Possibly three. All insulting her husband." He finished closing the distance between them and held her firmly against him. "So, Fox Girl, what happens now?"

"Mmm, now?" She moved her pelvis against him in a suggestive circle, loving the protective strength of his arms around her. "You mean right now or after we do the dishes?"

"Screw the dishes."

"Uh, no." She giggled and batted her lashes. "Screw *me*."

"Gladly." He unzipped her dress, stood back and let it slide to the floor, raised his brows when he saw her camisole with no bra underneath. "Oh, I like that. Very sexy."

"For you." She smiled, body heating up before he'd even started touching her in earnest.

"All for me." He stroked her breasts through the soft

cotton material, mouth curved, but not like his recent warm smiles, more like the way he'd been when she met him. Distant, disengaged. Something was up.

He moved her back a few steps until the top of her thighs made contact with the back of the couch. Then he knelt suddenly, lifted her dress, pulled her panties over her thigh-high stockings and assaulted her sex with his mouth.

She gasped, surprised by his attack, then her body turned on to the insistent thrusts of his tongue and she spread her legs wider, giving him access, feeling her face and body flush from the heat of her response. There was nothing tentative or hesitant about the way he touched her and it made her completely—

"Turn around." The order was curt, urgent.

She turned without question, heard him unzip, realized there would be no lingering tenderness this time. Was he angry? At her? Did he agree with her father that women should stay down and downtrodden?

Couldn't be. He'd seemed so happy for her.

The crinkle of foil, the hurried unrolling of latex, then one hand on her hip, guiding her, the other on her back, pushing her down over the couch. The initial thrust inside her, her gasp at how good it felt, then he settled into a strong rhythm.

Annabel braced her arms on the couch; her breasts swung forward and back with his lunges. For all her sexual excitement, she was slightly confused, slightly bewildered.

Until her senses registered his hands firmly holding her hips, and her brain pictured him standing behind her, huge, strong, impassive, moving her on and off him, hips thrusting, buttocks clenching, eyes narrow, jaw hard.

And she started to go wild.

He heard her moans, realized what she wanted and pushed harder. She must be tight in this position, she could feel him inside her so well, working her, in and out, hot friction.

One of her hands stayed on the couch to brace her, the other feverishly fumbled between her legs, found her clit and worked the familiar circle, bringing herself almost instantly to the brink of the orgasm his domination had her craving.

Annabel gave over to it, cried out and felt him clutch her hips, strain then stiffen and breathe in, then out, twice, steady and strong, and she knew he'd come, too and thrilled with him.

She collapsed down onto the couch, still joined to him, still wildly excited…and strangely disappointed. It was good sex. Great sex. Fabulous sex. But it wasn't sex with Quinn the way it had been last time. It was sex. Sex she could have had with any lover, though he excited her far beyond the others.

Not that she expected or wanted or needed all their lovemaking to be nothing but sweetness and tenderness. A little raunch once in a while was great, to keep things fresh, exciting.

But on their last night, when they were celebrating something really special…

Something was definitely up.

"Wow." She lifted onto her elbows, strained to turn and see if she could identify his mood from his expression. "That was…incredible."

"Yes." He pulled out, walked toward the bathroom. "Be right back."

O-kay. Annabel raised herself awkwardly to standing, feeling as if her muscles had temporarily frozen in the bent-over position. She pulled her panties up, stepped back into her dress and reached around to zip it. She did not want to be naked in front of him right now. She'd prefer a suit of armor, but the dress would have to do.

"You want to tell me what's wrong?" She spoke the second he reappeared in the living-room doorway, still trying to get the zipper past those pesky few inches in the middle of her back that were nearly impossible to reach.

"Nothing's wrong. You have to go down to Adolph's offices in Chicago in the morning, I have a plane to catch, it's late and we're both—"

"Quinn." She yanked at the zipper again, then gave up and let the dress flop open at the neckline. "Didn't you say we weren't allowed to pretend nothing was wrong when there was something?"

"Yes."

"And?"

His face softened. He walked over to her, threaded his hands in her hair and kissed her forehead. "The only thing wrong is that I'm leaving tomorrow. And once you sign on with Fox, between that and your business here, you and I officially become an impossibility for anything more than a once-a-year quickie, if that."

His words burst the last remaining bubble of Annabel's happiness, and a larger painful bubble—no, more like a lead cupcake—took its place. He didn't think their relationship could happen now. Was he trying to imply it was her fault? Or was she feeling guilty on her own?

"So you think I shouldn't take the job?"

"Did I say that?"

"No."

"If it's what you want, of course you should take it."

"If? *If* it's what I want?" She pulled away from his hands, part of her realizing she was arguing reflexively, that coming to care this much for Quinn *had* made her wonder whether high-powered success and all the 24/7 obsessions that came with it were really what she wanted.

But she couldn't stand the patronizing attitude that implied she might not really know what she wanted, that she might not be able to handle something this big and that they'd be better off if she rearranged *her* schedule to accommodate *their* needs.

N-n-n-nope.

"I've specifically said this is what I want. From the beginning."

"But this isn't the beginning anymore, Annabel. It's nearly the end."

"There must be a way we can—"

"I don't want to see you once a month for an hour." His voice raised and he paused for a long breath. "I want more than that. And believe me, the kind of schedule you're embarking on now isn't even going to afford us that one hour."

"So you think I should change my life goals so you and I can be together."

"No." He took a step back, looking so weary and grim that she took a comparable step forward to stay close to him. "That's not what I think."

"Then what do you think?"

He reached out, tucked a lock of hair behind her ear. "I think losing you will be one of the hardest things I've ever had to go through."

She gaped at him. Swallowed. And then tears came in a torrent, as if someone had found a way to stop Niagara Falls and someone else happened by and bumped the switch to On by mistake.

He put his arms around her, rocked her back and forth, and his tenderness only made her cry harder.

Get a grip, Annabel. Crying would solve nothing. She clung to him, fighting the tears with everything she had, and gradually brought herself under control. He held her another minute, then released her a little too fast for it to feel right or safe.

"You'd better go home. You'll need to sleep and it will only be harder for both of us if you stay until morning."

Annabel nodded dully, shocked at the pain that hit her. She'd counted on them having this one last night together. But he was right. There was no point staying, no point lying in bed next to each other all night, miserably waiting for the end.

Better leave now while things were relatively sweet, before either of them had a chance to think too hard, before the logical resentment could build, at the circumstances or at each other.

"The dishes." She gestured lamely at the mess, more than she could stand thinking about.

"I'll put away the food, soak the worst ones. Someone will be in tomorrow. I already arranged for them to clean up after the party so you wouldn't have to."

"Thank you." The tears wanted to come again, and again she fought them. "You are so good to me."

"It's what you deserve. Remember that." He walked with her to the door, handed her her coat, obviously wanting her out as fast as possible, to avoid a prolonged, agonizing scene. Probably just as well. She couldn't stand much more of this herself.

He put on his own coat and walked her out into the hall, down the elevator and to her car. Ever the gentleman, always watching out for her. Going back now to watching out for herself, as familiar as it was, would feel like a loss. God, she'd miss him. In one week he'd changed so much of her life.

"Good luck, Annabel. Stay in touch on e-mail. I'll call when I can."

She nodded, knowing they'd try for a while and then the futility of trying to recapture even a small part of the intimacy they'd established this week would overwhelm them, and they'd drift apart.

"Who knows. Maybe fifteen years from now we'll meet again."

She nodded again, unable to do anything else, then managed to croak out, "That would be nice," in the voice of a condemned woman.

"Merry Christmas, Annabel."

"Merry Christmas, Quinn," she whispered. Then she walked numbly around her van to the driver's side. Got in. Buckled. Started the engine. Pulled out. Saw him in her rearview mirror, standing on the curb watching her drive away.

This was the right thing to do. If she stayed in Milwaukee, if she turned down this opportunity to make time for him, she'd always wonder whether she could have had a better life, done bigger things, been someone. Time would vindicate her. She hoped it would. It had better.

Because right now she felt as if she'd made the worst, most completely wrong decision of her life.

ANNABEL WALKED off the elevators and down the empty beige corridor toward the Chicago branch of Adolph Fox's company, feeling as if the bad dream she'd had the night before was coming true. She'd been a ghostly figure, observing her own house while she was moving to Chicago for her new job. Friends and relatives, instead of packing, had been plundering her rooms for whatever they could carry away. Even Quinn was there, trying to pry away the kinky tiles around the fireplace to take home so he and his new love could practice different positions.

Then she'd been transported to Fox's company, a dark, foggy place, utterly silent until the Dolphster had sprung up out of the floor in a blaze of hellfire and shocked her awake.

Not happy thoughts. She'd had the nightmare shortly after she finally drifted off, and barely slept after that. Quinn might be out of her life, but missing him sat like a burning bowling ball in her chest. How long before she was over him? She *would* get over him, of course. People did. The human spirit was very resilient. And in the meantime, she'd have tons of exciting projects and new beginnings to distract her from the pain.

Right.

She reached the end of the hallway and massive wooden doors with huge round gold handles and the Adolph Fox & Company logo—his gold signature sprawled across a gold ladle.

Obviously, this was the place. Half-expecting the fires of hell, she opened the door and instead walked into a huge reception area—also beige—with a giant wooden desk front and center, behind which sat a gorgeous young woman dressed in—yes—beige, with honey-blond hair.

Was color not permitted in this company? Annabel felt positively loud in her black suit and red sweater. And not a Christmas decoration in sight. Not even on Christmas Eve.

Of course, um, she could think of someone else's office that wasn't exactly a rainbow, nor a seasonal masterpiece. She marched over to the receptionist, smiling politely. First chance she got, she was painting her office walls blue and buying a bright yellow chair. Maybe some colorful prints on the walls, too.

"I'm Annabel Brightman. I'm here to—"

"Yes." Ms. Receptionist smiled a fake, perfect white-toothed smile. "His secretary will be right out."

"Thank you." Annabel sent her a nice fake smile back and wondered if teeth-whitening strips were standard employee issue.

Ten seconds later, another stunning woman rounded the corner, also blond, this one wearing winter white.

Another fake smile. She introduced herself as Gina, then bent over to the receptionist. "Take my calls while I'm with Ms. Brightman."

"Okay, *Gina.*"

More baring of white teeth on both sides, oh my goodness, the meows were practically audible. What a lovely welcoming atmosphere.

"This way." Gina gestured down the beige hall.

Annabel fell into step beside her, expecting polite get-to-know-you conversation.

No polite get-to-know-you conversation.

The silence got weird.

"So, Gina, how long have you worked here?"

"Long enough." Gina pushed through a doorway into another office—ooh, light brown this time—and gestured to the table. "Just to get it out in the open, *I* was supposed to be the Fox Girl. Until you showed up."

"I see." Uh-oh. "So, you didn't have kitchen experience? Or..."

"I have kitchen experience." She pointed to a chair at the conference table and sank into the one opposite, folding her arms. "And I've been here since I graduated high school. I know the place inside out."

"Well. I'm...sorry. That must feel bad." Oh, this working relationship was going to be extra super special, Annabel could tell. With luck she wouldn't have to be in the office much.

"Whatever." Gina sent over a glance of sulky dislike. "Maybe you give better head than I do."

Annabel's eyelids snapped up like overwound shades. "*Excuse* me?"

Gina raised an eyebrow and took out a stack of folders. "Here's your schedule for the next month. If you sign on, you officially start January first."

"Wait a second." Annabel dumped her briefcase on the table and held up a hand like a traffic cop. "I am not sexually involved with Mr. Fox."

The other eyebrow went up. "Oh, please. We all know how it works around here. She gets to the top who bends over farthest and swallows the most."

"I have a boyfriend." For a second, after the words came out of her mouth, she desperately wanted it to be true. And she desperately wanted that boyfriend to be Quinn.

Gina shrugged. "So what's your point?"

"Are you saying I'll have to—"

The door to the room pushed open and *another* beautiful woman came in, older, maybe in her early thirties, and like the other two not a hair out of place. But at least her beige suit had a slight rose tint to it. She must be the radical in the bunch.

"Annabel, welcome, I'm Mr. Fox's assistant, Teresa."

Annabel stood and shook her hand, struck by the firmness of the other woman's grip and the complete lack of the announced welcome on her face. This was going to be a very, very, very long day. For a traitorous moment she thought of Stefanie, back at Annabel's comfortable house, holding down the fort, space heater blowing at her feet, miniature Christmas tree on her desk. Then Tanya's warm, homey shop, the garlands, the friendly customers, kids' pictures…

"I see Gina has given you your schedule. Thanks, Gina."

"You're welcome, Teresa."

Brr. Annabel resisted the urge to shiver. Battle of the Icy Bitches.

"Any questions so far, Ms. Brightman?"

"Please call me Annabel. Is Mr. Fox in today?" A friendly face would be a nice thing. A very nice thing.

The women exchanged glances.

"Yes."

The word came from both their perfectly made-up mouths at the same time, then they sat and stared.

"O-kay. Thank you." She sent them her umpteenth

fake smile of the day, wanting to be out of this room and back—

Yes. Okay. Right. Back in Milwaukee with Quinn? Who wasn't in Milwaukee anymore and since when had she been the type to run to a man when things got tough?

"Here is your contract." Another file was pushed across the table to her. "Should you decide to sign, you'd need to read it care—"

"Get a lawyer." Gina jumped and clamped her lips together. Annabel had the distinct impression Teresa had just kicked her under the table.

"Mr. Fox is looking for someone to represent the company with a more youthful look than he can provide. Specifically to appeal to the young men buying frozen food."

"Young *straight* men buying frozen food."

Annabel nodded and winked. "So I'll be a frozen-food prostitute?"

"Yes."

Again both women spoke together. Not the slightest attempt at a smile, fake or otherwise. Apparently humor wasn't allowed in here any more than color and Christmas.

The door swung open again, and the Dolphster himself strode in. Annabel stood. The women exchanged glances again, still seated, watching Annabel pointedly.

Oh, this was so comfy.

"Annabel, how nice to see you." He strode around the table, handsome in a black suit with a red tie, shooting off his usual energy and, instead of shaking her outstretched hand, to her horror, kissed it. Twice. "I'm delighted you're here. We can't wait to get started, can we, ladies?"

"No."

Both. Gina and Teresa. Zero enthusiasm.

"I have meetings set up for you all day today. Then off, of course, for Christmas. Then you can be back here the next day and—"

"Mr. Fox, I—"

"Uh-uh-uh…" He wiggled his index finger and glared at her coyly.

"Dolph." She didn't need to look at the women to see the glances exchanged that time. "I have my own business to run still in Milwaukee. I'd need to—"

"Ah, I understand. Well, you'll be able to take care of whatever you need to close that down."

"Close it down?" She gaped at him, horror rising. "You said nothing about—"

"Of course. I'll need you with me. There will be lots of travel involved, no way to keep your little business going with this schedule. Teresa, coffee. In my office."

Teresa got up, seething resentment. The Dolphster put his arm around Annabel's shoulders and led her out of the room. "Let's go discuss this in private, hmm?"

She let him lead her out, feeling Gina's hate rays boring into her back. This was so not what she had expected. This was like being invited to a fabulously elegant dinner party and being served moldy food. She and the big Dolph needed to have a little talk.

His office was large, lavish, unexpectedly colorful, the sills crowded with plants, framed posters of his products on the walls. His desk was immense, dark wood, neat piles of paper and folders, another plant that looked like silk.

He parked her in a chair and went around to sit on

his personal throne, accepted coffee from Teresa without thanks or eye contact and started rummaging in his middle drawer.

Annabel waited until Teresa had left the room, then took a deep breath. "Dolph, I have no idea of the polite way to say this, but it seems as if there's some misunderstanding among your staff of the role I'm going to be playing in this company."

He didn't look up. "I'm not following."

"To put it bluntly, they think I'm your mistress."

"Would you like to be?"

"Uh…" How did one turn down an offer so charming? He still hadn't looked up. "No, thank you."

"That's fine." He extracted two packages of sugar from somewhere in the back of his drawer and shook them to get the crystals to the bottom, finally meeting her eyes. "You are beautiful. I would love to have you, but I don't take women who are unwilling. Neither will I pester you—we have a business to run together, eh?"

Annabel tried not to slump in too obvious relief. "Thank you. That was weighing on me."

"Think nothing of it. I will set the girls straight."

Girls? Annabel couldn't help flinching, and at the same time wondering if any men were employed by Mr. Fox. Or unattractive women.

"Now. You have your schedule. You will meet people today, then we'll want to work on your look, do camera tests, photographs, make sure this will be as good a fit as I think it will be."

"Okay."

"Once the formalities are past, we'll be traveling two to three weeks of the month, especially around product-launch times and holidays. We do lectures, demonstrations—I like to be out and with the people as much as possible. That's what makes an impression. The personal touch, spending time with the ones who make the buying decisions, yes?"

Annabel nodded. Part of her was thrilled. This man knew how to work hard. He knew how to push and get what he wanted. She'd learn so much from him, get all the experience and exposure she needed to branch out effortlessly on her own someday.

At the same time, she now understood why he assumed she'd have to close Chefs Tonight. She thought of Stefanie and her students, out of jobs. Her clients having to cook for themselves until someone else came along.

And she could see the rest of her life getting swallowed up in a way she hadn't envisioned would ever be a problem until she met Quinn. Adolph Fox would be her constant companion facing a series of strange faces, cities, supermarkets, conference rooms and lecture halls.

Nothing like what she'd found with Quinn would be possible for her again.

And with that reality check, the last ray of hope that there would be some way to have her frozen cake and eat Quinn, too, was gone.

Her cell rang. She dug it out, glanced at the unfamiliar Wisconsin number and threw Adolph a questioning glance.

He spread his hands. "Business is business."

Annabel punched the phone on, trying not to think of Quinn insisting business should be pleasure.

"This is Frank." Stefanie's husband sounded strained, hoarse, nearly unrecognizable.

"Frank, what is it?"

"Stefanie's at Froedtert hospital." His voice shook. "They think she's going to lose the baby."

Annabel gasped; her stomach sank. "Baby?"

"You did this to her. You worked her so damn hard the whole time. Couldn't you see how tired she was?"

Annabel's jaw dropped. The rage and grief in his voice stunned her. "I didn't know she was pregnant."

"No, you didn't bother asking, did you."

"I *did*—" She stopped herself, feeling sick. He was right, in a way. She hadn't asked hard enough. "Is Stefanie okay?"

"I don't know. She started bleeding, then she collapsed. How could you be so cold? I hope you rot in hell for this."

The line clicked off. Annabel sat frozen, still pressing her phone to her ear. The logical part of her was telling her that miscarriages were common, that they were caused many times by the fetus not being viable. That working as hard as Stefanie had wouldn't be enough to hurt her or the baby. That Frank was obviously scared and that fear had turned to anger and Annabel was the obvious target.

The rest of her felt like absolute donkey dung.

"Bad news?"

Annabel nodded, managing to get the phone down from her ear and power it off, stuff it back in her purse. "A friend is miscarrying."

"Sorry to hear that. Those things are hard." He nodded, seeming genuinely sympathetic, then clapped his hands together. "Now. Where were we?"

For ten more minutes, Annabel listened to him dic-

tate how her life would go. Half listened. The rest of her
was in the hospital with Stefanie. She wanted to be there
with her. Not that there was anything she could do. Not
that she felt she'd really caused her to lose the baby.

But because she was important. And Annabel, for once,
needed to take the time to make sure Stefanie knew it.

Adolph pressed a buzzer on his desk, summoned a
visibly hostile Teresa and gave her orders for transpor-
tation and lunch.

Annabel blinked and focused on him. Is that how she
was going to end up? Hated and alone? Was that the
kind of future she was building for herself?

It might have been. If she hadn't met Quinn.

She stood and picked up her purse. Adolph looked
up in surprise. "Where are you going?"

"To see my friend."

His salt-and-pepper brows lowered. "I have meetings
booked for you all day, Annabel."

"I realize that. But she needs me."

He scoffed. "What the hell can you do, save this baby?"

"No, but I can be there for her."

He gestured in frustration, let his hand slam down on
the desk. "What the hell priorities are these?"

"Good ones." She laughed, a little hysterically. "Finally."

"You can't just walk away."

"Surprisingly…mostly to me—" she shouldered her
purse and looked him straight in the eye "—I can."

She swept out of the room, out of the contract, out
of an opportunity that would have given her everything
she thought she wanted.

And very little she actually did.

13

QUINN STOOD on his mother's back porch nursing a glass of wine, breath coming out frosty white in the bitter air. In front of him, the snow-and-pine-covered hills rose and fell in the distance; the afternoon sun shone weakly, already on its way down to early darkness. Inside, his mother napped, while the traditional Garrett Christmas Eve out-of-the-freezer meal of rich turkey soup made from Thanksgiving leftovers warmed gently on the stove. From Milwaukee, he'd brought French bread and some imported cheeses to go with it. Red wine. Just ripe d'Anjou pears. And a chocolate torte with enough calories per slice to keep a small village fed for a day.

The soup represented their humble beginnings, their dedication to family traditions. The cheese and wine and chocolate were Quinn's way of saying, yeah, but let's not forget life can be good, too.

Except right now life didn't feel good. Would every meal he cooked from now on remind him of Annabel? Every second spent in the kitchen bring on painful memories?

He pictured her, trotting after Adolph Fox, hungry for everything he'd teach her, pumped up by the thrill of achieving the pinnacle of her dreams. But how long would that thrill last? How long was Napoleon content with each conquest before the hunger started in again? Had she thought about him this morning or wavered on the way to Chicago? He'd like to think so. Hell, he'd like to hear her voice on the phone telling him it was all a mistake.

But that had to be her move to make. No more manipulation from him. Nor was he going to whine at her to give him another chance. She'd made her choice, and he had to live with it.

At least now he knew he could fall in love, that there were women out there he could think about making a life with. Before this, he honestly hadn't been sure if he had the ability in him, or if he would spend the rest of his life with occasional women and his billions. If there was Annabel, there had to be more like her. Right? Other fish in the sea?

He tossed the rest of his excellent red wine out into the snow, where it made a bloodlike crevice. Crap, all of it. He was hooked on her. By the time he managed to fall out of love with Annabel Brightman, if it were even possible, he'd probably be too old to get it up anymore. She'd brought him out of the careful coffin of his existence, brought him alive again, and now it hurt like hell to be going back six feet under with the memory of what real life felt like.

The cold started pinching his ears and nose; he turned and went back inside. The house smelled like pine and turkey and herbs; it was warm and comforting and he told himself to cheer the hell up. No room for grumps on Christmas Eve. He had everything he wanted materially, his mom was healthy and happy, there were presents under the tree, good food on the stove and in the refrigerator. Time to be grateful for what he had instead of moaning over what he'd lost.

He rolled his eyes and shut the sliding porch door behind him. Yeah, nice try. That crap didn't work, either.

Fighting gloom, he strode into his room, now officially the guest room, and booted up his laptop to check e-mail.

To: Quinn Garrett
From: John Brightman
Date: December 24
Subject: Merry Christmas
Hi Quinn. Just wanted to say Merry Christmas. I'm sorry you weren't able to spend it with us here, but I understand. Our house is always open. Let us know your schedule and we'll be really glad to see you anytime.

Must run, the kids are losing their minds as they do every year. But I wanted to know if you knew what was going on with Annabel. She doesn't seem quite herself, and not in a good way. She's usually pretty open about what's going on, but this time I got nowhere. Of course I'm worried about her.

Hope you are well.

John

Quinn scanned his e-mail for anything else important, putting his emotions deliberately on hold. Finding nothing, he closed the program and allowed himself to react. First came the surge of concern. Second came frustration. Why the hell was Annabel putting them through this if they were both miserable? Third, un-willingly, came hope. Maybe she was unhappy enough to change her mind?

No, he couldn't think that way. Unless he heard it out of her mouth, there was no point creating a fantasy and allowing himself to be carried off.

He shut down the laptop and put it away, rummaged in the case for his cell. One message. Annabel's num-ber. His heart started pounding. He punched into his voice mail and put the phone to his ear. The message had come in shortly before noon.

"It's Annabel." Her voice sounded thick, uneasy. "I'm…on my way home now. And I'll be there tomor-row if you want to call. Merry Christmas. Bye."

He blew out a long breath, tried again to rid himself of the rush of protectiveness. She'd sounded down. Un-certain. Not herself, exactly as John sensed. And going home from Chicago that early? Though, of course, it was Christmas Eve.

So what now? Call full of hope only to find out she was having a lonely moment. Maybe the first morning with Dolph had overwhelmed her, but that was all? Or she just wanted to hear his voice? Then what? They'd chat politely, wish each other Merry Christmas and hope things were going well?

God no, he couldn't stand that. He wanted so damn much more. Worse, he was barely hanging on to the last little thread of his pride by not rushing to call her back. By not hopping into his plane and attempting one more time to carry her off to his castle. Or bringing his cas-tle to her via the R and D facility in Milwaukee as he'd thought of doing more and more frequently until Adolph had shown up with his offer. She could snip even that last little bit.

"Quinn." His mother emerged from her bedroom, still using a walker until her hip healed completely. Her cheery welcoming smile dimmed as she searched his face. "Time for drinks, isn't it?"

"Anytime you're ready is time for drinks, Mom." He got up from his old desk, kissed her forehead and helped her into the living room and onto the sofa. "Want me to light a fire?"

"Sure. But drinks first. When you're as old as I am, you gotta have priorities."

Quinn grinned and went to the kitchen, poured her a sherry and one for himself, though he didn't much care for the stuff. And halfway through that first glass of wine he'd already known alcohol was a bad idea in this mood.

He brought the sherry back to his mother, put his down on the coffee table and squatted by the woodstove, laying the newspaper, bits of old shingles and birch logs that would make the cozy evening seem complete.

Yet all he could think about was how only Annabel could make it truly complete for him. He was turning into a miserable excuse for a—

"So are you going to stay here dutifully with your old mother and be a complete pathetic sap the whole holiday or are you going to fly back to Milwaukee and spend Christmas with her like you really want to?"

Quinn stayed where he was, struck a match, lit the newspaper, watched the flame spread along the printed words, turning them brown and brittle. "I'm staying with you."

"Oh, good choice." His mother made a scornful

noise. "I'll be fine here, son. Hank is coming over later. He and I have had some lovely Christmasses together. And with you out of the way we can get naked."

Quinn laughed, rose to his feet and looked at his mom tenderly. "Is that right."

"Seriously." She blinked back, utterly guileless. "You'd be doing us a favor."

He sat next to her on the sofa, took up his sherry glass and toasted her. "Thanks, Mom. But I think I'll stay anyway."

"Suit yourself." She clinked his glass, took a healthy gulp and pointed to the tree. "Your present for tonight is the red round one. Open it now."

"Okay." He got up again and searched the pile of wrapped gifts. During his childhood, his mom always allowed one present on Christmas Eve, since he'd been too excited to wait until the next morning. They'd kept up the tradition for whatever reason.

The round red present was nestled to one side. He picked it up and also the box of ridiculously expensive hot-chocolate mix he had brought his mother, who liked her cocoa as strong as coffee and nearly as bitter.

She opened hers first, exclaiming over the chocolate as if it were the crown jewels. Moms were so good that way.

He opened his carefully, pleased smile already in place. An ornament emerged from the wrapping, clear glass carefully painted with a blue-green swirling design and a dove, olive branch in its beak, soaring through the abstract sky. Printed around the top, in careful teenage handwriting, "To Quinn. Merry Christmas. With Love, Annabel."

Quinn looked over the top of the ornament, through

the bright haze that seemed to be covering his eyes, his arm still held up high as if it had frozen. "Where did you get this?"

As soon as he asked, he knew. He'd brought it home that year, wrapped it carefully in tissue paper, tucked it in a shoebox and hid it high in his closet where no human ever ventured.

"I found it years ago, after you went to college and your father left, when I was cleaning. In a box, along with an old dried-up sprig of mistletoe and a Valentine it looks like you never sent her. I thought it was time you saw it again. Couldn't decide at first whether to give it to you like this, or hang it on the tree, or just bash you over the head with it and hope you came to your senses."

Quinn stared at the ornament. The swirls Annabel had painted danced, and the bird flew joyously over the surface of the glass, bringing the plain brittle surface to warm life. The same way she'd brought him to it.

The longing for her became so painful that he stood abruptly, unable to sit there and take it anymore.

His mother peered up at him, love and pride sparkling in her faded brown eyes. "Going somewhere, dear? I hope?"

He shook his head, chuckling at his own idiocy. Who the hell was he kidding? He'd been in love with Annabel since he was seventeen years old, and he wasn't going to give her up now, no matter how long it took, no matter how many kicks in the teeth she dealt him, no matter how much deprivation he had to suffer for each precious minute he spent with her. He'd come alive in the last week and he wasn't going to let any of that life go to waste.

"Yes." He grinned sheepishly at his mother, adrenaline and joy sparking through him. "I'm going."

ANNABEL WEDGED her van between two SUVs in the Froedtert hospital parking garage. She'd miraculously arrived at Union Station in Chicago only fifteen minutes before a train scheduled for Milwaukee, so she was here barely two hours after Frank had called. She'd tried twice to call him back, but he hadn't answered her message. Which wasn't good.

Not knowing if Stefanie and her baby were okay was killing her. The guilt that even in some tiny way she might have caused the problem was killing her. The unprofessionalism of walking out on Adolph Fox on her first day there was killing her. Not really caring was killing her more. Not being able to see Quinn was killing her triple.

Frankly, this was not her best day.

She raced into the E.R., questioned the nurse on duty, found out Stefanie was up in Labor and Delivery, and made her way to the adjacent building. Good that Stefanie wasn't still in the E.R. Bad that she was still in the hospital. Down the corridor into the elevator up to the sixth floor, out and to the right as directed.

Incredibly, she bumped into Frank and Stefanie just leaving the unit, Stefanie walking on her own steam, both of them smiling at a piece of paper as if it were the Holy Grail.

Oh, thank God. Annabel stopped and put a hand to the wall to support her body's wilt into relief. This did not look like a couple who had just lost a baby. Oh, thank God.

"Annabel." Stefanie stared in surprise. "What are you doing here?"

"Frank called me." She glanced at him and noted his averted-eyes mortification. Apparently he'd overreacted. She didn't care. All she cared about was that Stefanie was okay. Which sort of amazed and delighted her, because she'd just blown off the biggest career move of her life, and this proved it had been the right decision. Otherwise, she'd have wanted to remove Frank's dialing finger with a blunt instrument.

"You called her? Why on earth did you call her?" Stefanie practically shrieked at her husband. "Frank…she's my boss."

Frank opened his mouth, stared at the floor, scratched his short punky hair. "I thought she—"

"I'm your friend, Stefanie. Frank knew I'd want to know if there was any danger."

Stefanie's eyes narrowed. "There wasn't any danger. I have anemia which is why I've been so tired. And when I saw the bleeding, which turned out to be nothing, I had an anxiety attack and fainted. Frank sort of—"

"I freaked out." He met Annabel's eyes with his long-lashed dark ones. "I thought she was miscarrying, or something worse. Everyone did. I lost it. I'm sorry."

"Please don't tell me you came back from Chicago for this." Stefanie's expression clearly indicated torture in store for Frank if the answer was yes.

"No. I was done." More true than they realized.

"Whew." Stefanie smiled and extended the piece of paper she and Frank had been gazing at. "This is our baby."

Annabel peered at the grainy white-and-gray blob

and tried very hard to figure out what part of it could possibly be a baby. "Wow. That's…wow."

"We saw the heartbeat and everything. Imagine, something that small and already its heart is beating." Stefanie blinked back tears and Frank put his arm around her and squeezed tight, looking as if he was about to join her crying.

Annabel took in a sharp breath and held it against a sudden powerful longing. She wanted this. A man who loved her so much he was willing to lose his mind and shout accusations at someone he barely knew. A baby that was part of both of them, that would bind them into a family, the warm, loving unit that Annabel herself had grown up in and Quinn still needed to experience.

"I'm…sorry I didn't tell you sooner I was pregnant." Stefanie bit her lip, sharing her husband's previous fascination with the floor.

Annabel glanced at Frank, then warmly at the top of Stefanie's head. "I think I know why you didn't. But it's wonderful news. We'll need to talk about maternity leave. Oh, and maybe you can leave the baby with Kathy across the street while you're at work. If…you want to keep working."

"You're not going to close the business now that you're with Mr. Fox?"

Annabel smiled, took a deep breath of antiseptic hospital air and spoke the words she'd probably known were true the day she walked out of Quinn's apartment and left him behind, thinking she'd seen the end of their relationship.

Which, unbelievably, was only yesterday.

"I won't be working for Mr. Fox."

There. She had said it. And the hospital hadn't jarred and rumbled and fallen to the ground in a cloud of ash and cement and steel. The sun was still shining. Or most likely it was—there wasn't a window in sight here.

More importantly, a wave of joy swelled so big inside her she felt like the Grinch, his new big-sized heart busting out the sides of the magnifying glass. Or Scrooge, coming home from his visits with the three spirits to realize he still had a future ahead to live so much more wisely and warmly than his past.

She hugged Stefanie, shook Frank's big hand awkwardly and accepted the apology in his eyes. She didn't blame him. From now on Annabel was going to be different. Different! She wished them both a Merry Christmas and hurried down the corridor, barely resisting the urge to kick up her heels.

Out of the hospital, into the sunny chill of a beautiful Christmas Eve afternoon. Christmas! She drove toward home as fast as she could without risking a ticket, then impulsively turned into the Sentry parking lot. Ten minutes later, she emerged with wrapping paper, gift tags and a large fresh turkey and piled it into the back of her van.

Home.

She drove into the garage and hefted the bird and wrapping items to her back door, burst into her house and immediately hated the emptiness and the chill.

First things first. She turned the heat way up, then took off her coat, picked up the phone and called her cousin.

"Linda, it's Annabel."

"Annabel!" She sounded as if she was happier to

hear from Annabel than anything that had ever happened to her.

"I'd love to come to your party tomorrow, if the invitation still stands."

"You—" Linda broke off, apparently unable to cope with the shock. Then she whispered something, probably to Evan. Perhaps instructing him to contact a psychiatrist.

Annabel grinned. Ha! Take that! She was transformed! Into a warm bundle of Christmas pudding. And once she called Quinn, that Christmas pudding would have rum poured over it and be set alight.

"We'd love to have you, darling. I'm so pleased you'll be coming!"

"See you at four?"

"Yes. Annabel, I'm really looking forward to it."

"Me, too." She giggled as she hung up, surprised to find it was really the truth. Oh, this felt so good.

Next call. She rummaged through her address book and came up with the sheet of neighbor phone numbers. Kathy…whatever her last name was. She scanned the list. Kathy…and Joseph Jablonski. There. Dialing…

"Kathy, it's Annabel. I'm calling to see if you still need a replacement turkey tonight at the block party."

"Well, we were going to do fine without it, but it's always such a nice centerpiece. Why?"

"It's already bought, I'll get it in the oven this second."

"Well…I…" Kathy finally managed to splutter out her surprised thanks and Annabel grinned.

"You're welcome. It's the least I can do."

She rang off the phone, then hurried into the kitchen. There she trussed the turkey, rubbed it with butter, olive oil and herbes de Provence, stuffed it with onions and lemons and more herbs, then got it into the preheated oven. Done. What next?

Too late to shop for her clients, but she knew a site where she could send e-cards with gift certificates they could redeem from any of a large number of merchants. Why hadn't she thought of doing this before?

Because she hadn't met Quinn yet. Because she'd been a one-track automaton, full only of herself and her own goals. Because the milk of human kindness had only just started flowing. Of course since this next out-pouring was for her clients, she had to provide regular, low-fat, skim, lactose-free and soy.

She burst into her office, imagining the walls blue, turned on her computer, sent the cards and certificates to all her clients and shut the machine down. Her eyes lit on an old message that had gotten wedged into the corner of her keyboard tray. What was this? Ah! The or-ganization that had wanted her to do cooking demon-strations for kids. Of course she'd do it. She'd be glad to do it. It would be a blast.

She called and left a message, then rummaged in her purse for the right business card, called Bob's fiancée, Karen, wished her a very merry Christmas and said she was ready to go ahead with the Web site design after the holiday.

Okay.

Now. She took a deep breath. Stood. Sat. Stood again. The most important part of making things right.

Quinn.

She'd left him a nervous message earlier, when she had first heard from Frank and was on her way back to Milwaukee. Somewhat ominously, he hadn't called back, though she'd left it open that he could call her Christmas Day. Maybe he was busy with his mother. Maybe he hadn't checked his messages. Maybe he decided he was done with her and her c'mere, e'mere, go away, go away attitude.

Well, that was all in the past. She wanted him to c'mere forever. She wanted to find a way they could forge some kind of relationship around their busy schedules. She wanted…him.

She grabbed her phone again, dialed his cell number. Left another message and hung up feeling deflated and a little nervous. Well, of course being able to reach him, having him say yes, I love you, come to me now my darling, would be the perfect climax to her personal epiphany, but life had a way of screwing up perfect moments with its own plans, didn't it.

Okay. She could…well, what? Tomorrow was Christmas. She wanted to give him something, even if it would be a day or two late. Just having something wrapped under the tree tomorrow that would eventually belong to him would bring him closer. She wanted to give him *her* for Christmas, but she didn't think express delivery would take her to Maine overnight.

For a crazy second she thought of flying up to see him, but all she knew was that his mother lived in Hartland, and it was very possible she wouldn't welcome Annabel busting up her chance to celebrate a holiday with her only child.

So. What? She had a couple of hours until the turkey was ready. Stores were open. Maybe she could still find the perfect gift.

Two hours later, she came back from Mayfair Mall

with baby clothes for Stefanie and Frank. Nothing remotely right enough for Quinn, darn it. She'd just have to talk to him. Right now it was time to take the turkey out, let it rest, then go the block party.

Turkey out, oven off, she went upstairs for a quick shower and changed into black linen pants and a red sweater. What more? She suddenly remembered a miniature Christmas-tree pin her father had given her, which she hadn't worn in years, and managed to find it in an old jewelry box. Perfect. And?

She had just opened the bottom drawer of the beautiful tortoiseshell miniature dresser in search of a pair of faux-diamond-and-gold earrings, when into her head clicked the absolutely perfect gift idea for Quinn.

A FEW MINUTES before twelve, Annabel left the block party. To her complete and utter surprise, she'd had a really nice time, if she didn't count the fact that her insides were being regularly seared with longing for Quinn. But her neighbors were very friendly and interesting people. She'd even gotten a few possible requests for her services. What did they say about finding happiness in your own backyard? Maybe she needed to concentrate less on the wealthy and more on average working moms. Devise some budget menus and see how those flew. She kind of liked the idea of being a local champion of the working mother. Maybe that would be a nice angle to try.

Snow had started falling earlier in the evening, and already about an inch covered the ground, six to eight total expected by morning, according to the guests at the party.

A nearby church bell started to chime midnight. It

was Christmas. She let herself into the chilly dark foyer through her front door, thinking how Adolph Fox and his world seemed so far away. And damn it, so did Quinn. Maybe she should call him again. Just to see if—

She pushed open the inner door into her living room and froze.

Her tree glowed beautiful colors in the dark living room. She was sure she hadn't turned it on before she left. A beautiful blazing fire provided the only other light. She was *quite* sure she hadn't built that.

"Merry Christmas, Annabel."

Her ears registered him first, then her breath, catching in her throat, and her heart, racing to impossible speeds. Then her muscles kicked in. She turned and her eyes got the best present she could possibly, possibly have.

"I kept this." Quinn walked over to her and pushed a copy of her house key into her hand. "You should have it back."

She shook her head. "You keep it."

His brows went up. "For?"

"For when you visit me?"

"How often will that be possible?"

"Whenever you can. I'll be here."

His eyes lit with hope. "What about Adolph?"

"No more Adolph." The words sounded so good. "It's not what I really wanted."

"What do you really want?" He put his hands to her waist, drew her close, so much warmth and what she damn well hoped was love on his face, that she could barely speak.

"I really want you to open your present."

He looked a little startled, not that she could blame him. "Okay."

She darted to the tree, picked up his present and stopped in her tracks. A new ornament hung on a prominent branch, the one she had made for him all those years ago. "You kept this?"

"Yes." He grinned the grin she'd missed like mad, the one that made him look so boyish and full of life. "Does that tell you something?"

"I think so." She handed him his present, suddenly understanding what people meant when they said their hearts were in their throats. "My turn to tell you something."

He slid off the wrapping paper and looked questioningly at the dresser. "Back at me?"

"Open it."

"Keys?"

"Not locked."

"All the drawers the same?"

"All different."

He watched her carefully, trying to get into her mind with his patented Quinn ability. "Is my fate being decided here?"

"I hope so," she whispered.

He gazed at her a second longer, then opened the bottom drawer, took out a tiny green Christmas tree she'd cut from a gift tag and folded, which opened to show the word *You.*

"Me?"

"Open more."

Top drawer next, a red-and-white Santa with the word *I* written on his hat.

"I...you." He tapped on the middle drawer. "Does this have the word *want* in it?"

She shook her head, trying to keep the nerves and excitement off her face.

"Need?"

"No."

"Maim?"

She laughed. "Oh, no."

He pulled open the drawer and took out the gold star. He stared at it for a long, long time, then put it down carefully and pulled her into his arms. "I love you, too, Annabel. I have for a very long time."

He kissed her. The kisses turned wild and passionate and they undressed each other, sank to the floor and made slow, beautiful, languid love facing each other on their sides, toe to toe, cheek to cheek and everything in between, firelight dancing over their bodies, the tile couples no doubt looking on approvingly.

Afterward, she lay in his arms, happier than she could ever remember being, not even minding the rough rug under her. They might not be able to see a lot of each other, but when they did, they'd make every second count.

Quinn stroked her hair and cleared his throat. "I've decided to turn the Milwaukee building into an R and D facility."

"Oh?" She murmured the word sleepily into his chest, her other senses so full of him she barely registered the words.

"And I'm going to give up being CEO and move to Milwaukee to run it."

"Mmm—huh?" She launched herself off his chest and stared at his gorgeous face in the firelight. "You are?"

He grinned at her. "Yes."

"You're changing your entire life for me?"

"Yes. And because it's what I want. Did you change yours for me?"

"Yes." She laughed, put her hands to her temples, hardly able to believe it. Quinn would be here. They'd have time for each other. Time to see if this relationship would turn into forever as much as she felt in her bones it would. "And because it's what I wanted for me, too."

He pulled her back down beside him. "I never thought I'd have the luxury of asking you this, Annabel. But what do you want to do tomorrow? Besides make love in more positions than those fireplace guys could ever dream of?"

"Hmm." She glanced out the window at the snow still coming down. "Maybe we could go out and make a snowman?"

"Frosty?"

"Siegfried."

He chuckled. "Let's run and have some fun now?"

"Yes." She reached to his face, kissed him, feeling the love and passion flaring again between them, feeling with every bone in her body that it always would. "Before we melt away."

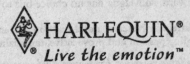

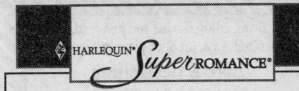

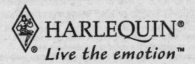

If you enjoyed what you just read,
then we've got an offer you can't resist!

Take 2 bestselling
love stories FREE!

Plus get a FREE surprise gift!

Clip this page and mail it to Harlequin Reader Service®

IN U.S.A.
3010 Walden Ave.
P.O. Box 1867
Buffalo, N.Y. 14240-1867

IN CANADA
P.O. Box 609
Fort Erie, Ontario
L2A 5X3

YES! Please send me 2 free Blaze™ novels and my free surprise gift. After receiving them, if I don't wish to receive anymore, I can return the shipping statement marked cancel. If I don't cancel, I will receive 4 brand-new novels each month, before they're available in stores! In the U.S.A., bill me at the bargain price of $3.99 plus 25¢ shipping and handling per book and applicable sales tax, if any*. In Canada, bill me at the bargain price of $4.47 plus 25¢ shipping and handling per book and applicable taxes**. That's the complete price and a savings of at least 10% off the cover prices—what a great deal! I understand that accepting the 2 free books and gift places me under no obligation ever to buy any books. I can always return a shipment and cancel at any time. Even if I never buy another book from Harlequin, the 2 free books and gift are mine to keep forever.

150 HDN DZ9K
350 HDN DZ9L

Name	(PLEASE PRINT)	
Address	Apt.#	
City	State/Prov.	Zip/Postal Code

Not valid to current Harlequin Blaze™ subscribers.

Want to try two free books from another series?
Call 1-800-873-8635 or visit www.morefreebooks.com.

* Terms and prices subject to change without notice. Sales tax applicable in N.Y.
** Canadian residents will be charged applicable provincial taxes and GST.
 All orders subject to approval. Offer limited to one per household.
 ® and ™ are registered trademarks owned and used by the trademark owner or its licensee.

BLZ04R   ©2004 Harlequin Enterprises Limited.

The world's bestselling romance series.

HARLEQUIN®
Presents

Seduction and Passion Guaranteed!

GREEK TYCOONS

They're the men who have everything—except a bride....

Wealth, power, charm—what else could a heart-stoppingly
handsome tycoon need? In the GREEK TYCOONS
miniseries you have already been introduced to some
gorgeous Greek multimillionaires who are in need of wives.

THE GREEK BOSS'S DEMAND
by *Trish Morey*
On sale January 2005, #2444

THE GREEK TYCOON'S
CONVENIENT MISTRESS
by *Lynne Graham*
On sale February 2005, #2445

THE GREEK'S
SEVEN-DAY SEDUCTION
by *Susan Stephens*
On sale March 2005, #2455

Pick up a Harlequin Presents® novel and you will enter a world
of spine-tingling passion and provocative, tantalizing romance!

Available wherever Harlequin books are sold.

www.eHarlequin.com